City Under the Stars

ALSO BY GARDNER DOZOIS

SELECTED BIBLIOGRAPHY

Nightmare Blue (with George Alec Effinger)
Strangers (as Gardner R. Dozois)
Hunter's Run (with Daniel Abraham and George R. R. Martin)

COLLECTIONS

The Visible Man
Slow Dancing Through Time
Geodesic Dreams: The Best Short Fiction of Gardner Dozois
Morning Child and Other Stories
When the Great Days Come

AS EDITOR

Best Science Fiction Stories of the Year (volumes 6–10)
Under African Skies
Under South American Skies
The Good Old Stuff: Adventure SF in the Grand Tradition
The Good New Stuff: Adventure SF in the Grand Tradition

The Good Stuff
Isaac Asimov's Science Fiction (magazine) (1986–2004)
Old Mars (with George R. R. Martin)
Old Venus (with George R. R. Martin)
The Exclamatory Series (with Jack Dann)
The Year's Best Science Fiction (volumes 1–35)
Warriors (with George R. R. Martin) (volumes 1–3)
plus many more anthologies, far too numerous to list

NONFICTION

The Fiction of James Tiptree, Jr.
Writing Science Fiction and Fantasy (with Tina Lee, Stanley Schmidt, Ian Randal Strock, and Sheila Williams)
Sense of Wonder: Short Fiction Reviews (2009–2017)
Strange Days: Fabulous Journeys with Gardner Dozois

ALSO BY MICHAEL SWANWICK

SELECTED BIBLIOGRAPHY

THE IRON DRAGONS SERIES

The Iron Dragon's Daughter

The Dragons of Babel

The Iron Dragon's Mother

In the Drift

Vacuum Flowers

Stations of the Tide

Jack Faust

Bones of the Earth

Dancing with Bears

Chasing the Phoenix

COLLECTIONS

Gravity's Angels

A Geography of Unknown Lands

Tales of Old Earth

Moon Dogs

The Dog Said Bow-Wow

The Best of Michael Swanwick
Not So Much, Said the Cat
The Postmodern Adventures of Darger and Surplus
Puck Aleshire's Abecedary
Cigar-Box Faust and Other Miniatures
Michael Swanwick's Field Guide to the Mesozoic Megafauna
The Periodic Table of Science Fiction

NONFICTION

The Postutopian Archipelago
What Can Be Saved from the Wreckage?: James Branch Cabell in the Twenty-First Century
Hope-in-the-Mist: The Extraordinary Career and Mysterious Life of Hope Mirrlees
Being Gardner Dozois (an interview)

CITY UNDER THE STARS

GARDNER DOZOIS
AND MICHAEL SWANWICK

A TOM DOHERTY ASSOCIATES BOOK
NEW YORK

This is a work of fiction. All of the characters, organizations, and events portrayed in this novella are either products of the author's imagination or are used fictitiously.

CITY UNDER THE STARS

Cover art by Raphael Lacoste
Cover design by Christine Foltzer

Edited by Ellen Datlow and Lee Harris

The first part of this book was first published in
OMNI 1995 as *The City of God.*

A Tordotcom Book
Published by Tom Doherty Associates
120 Broadway
New York, NY 10271

www.tor.com

ISBN 978-1-250-75657-2 (ebook)
ISBN 978-1-250-75658-9 (trade paperback)

First Edition: August 2020

As coauthor of this book, I would like to dedicate my half
TO THE MEMORY OF GARDNER DOZOIS
who, I know, intended to dedicate his half
TO THE MEMORY OF SUSAN CASPER
but who, had he lived just a little longer,
would almost certainly have added
AND TO ARABEL

City Under the Stars

1

IT WAS HIGH SUMMER in Orange, in York, in the Human Domain of Earth. There was commerce in the town, crops in the field, beasts in the byre, bandits in the roads, thants and chimeras in the hills, and God in His Heaven—which was fifteen miles away, due east.

From where Hanson worked—on an open platform extending out from the side of the giant State Factory of Orange and nestling right up against the bare, rocky face of Industry Hill—it was possible to look east, out across the teeming squalor of Orange, and see the Wall of the City of God marching north-south across the horizon, *making* the horizon really: a radiant line drawn across the misty blue of distance, pink as a baby's thigh, pink as dawn. And to know that it stretched, in all its celestial arrogance, more than two hundred miles to the north, and more than three hundred miles to the south, unbroken, cutting three-quarters of the Human Domain off from the sea—the City of God, perfect and inviolable, with a completeness that was too much for man. That was what Hanson must face every day when he came to work and stood in the sun and in his human sweat with his little shovel. That terrible, alien beauty, indifferent to mortality, forever at his back, a head's turn away, as he worked, as he grew old. And knowing that God and all the angels were in there, pure and incomprehensible as fire, maybe watching him right now, looking down over the Edge of the Wall and into the finite world: a huge watery eye, tall as the sky.

But no one ever thought much about God on shift, not for long. The sun was too hot in summer, the wind too bitter in winter, the work killing in any season, blighting and shriveling a man, draining him dry. There was too much sickness, not enough food, little medicine, little comfort, and only brief bitter joys. It soon became evident that God didn't care about man, that He paid no more attention to the misery swarming beneath the Wall of His City than man pays to the activities of beetles, that He had no more compassion for humanity's messy agonies than man had for the suffering and tribulations of mayflies. There were two State Temples of Purified Catholicism visible in the sweep below, and even the encircled cross that marked a *kachina* shrine, a *kiva*, but none of them were very well attended. In spite of its proximity to the Wall of the City of God—or perhaps because of it—Orange was not a devoutly religious town.

Hanson leaned into his shovel and watched the blade

disappear into the coal. The pile sloped up and back, toward the lips of the gullet, through which new lumps of coal would rattle slowly down onto the top of the heap every few seconds, obliging the shift to keep up a steady tempo of work to avoid being swamped. On heavy days they would have to shovel like fiends to keep up, dumping the coal down chutes into hoppers on the lower transport level of the factory. But no matter how much they sweated, the coal remained undiminished, replenished constantly from the top as fast as they could clear it away from the bottom: a glossy black mountain crawling sluggishly with the unending inching motion of the coal. Hanson had even stopped hating it, regarding it now as a condition to be endured, something too big, impersonal, and constant to rail against, impersonal as a thunderstorm. His mother had told him an ancient tale once—a few months before she'd died in one of the food riots that were an aftermath of the Campaign Against the South—about women with brooms trying to sweep the sea free of salt. He often thought about the tale while on shift, and unlimbered the flinty thing that had served him for a smile the past few years, since his wife, Becky, had died coughing blood in the White Winter four seasons back.

It seemed that everyone he had ever known and loved had died, one by one over the falling years, leaving him here in the barren center of nothing, living on and on, alone. He had never wanted it that way. He'd never asked for that.

Taking a step backward, Hanson scooped up a shovelful of coal, pivoted smoothly, and tossed it over the curb and into the chute, turning back for another shovelful without bothering to watch the first fall. After years on the job, he could send a steady stream of coal anywhere he wanted it, with pinpoint accuracy, almost without looking. He placed his foot on the blade, dug it back into the pile, and stopped. Normally he would work like this for hours without stopping, steady as a mechanical thing, his motions flowing into an unbroken cycle. But today—today he could not keep his mind on his job, today he was like a child, distracted by anything, everything, the wind, the sky, the light glinting from his shovel blade. He leaned on the shovel, buried up to the handle in the pile, and watched the gullet spit up some more coal.

Somewhere up there, miles deep into the slope, miles beneath Industry Hill, maybe even halfway to Pitt, one of the last surviving Utopian autominers was burrowing and wallowing like a steel whale through a deep vein of coal, exploring the secret roots of the world. No—it was blind, and ate its way past wonders it could never see, so maybe tapeworm would be a better analogy than whale:

a robotic, reactor-powered tapeworm that gnawed through Earth's bowels with adamantine teeth, insatiably tracing the tightening convolutions of the intestines, passing the ore through its indestructible body and voiding it back along the endless tail of the conveyor field to the mouth of the gullet. Where it dribbled onto the pile and tumbled slowly down the grade so that Hanson or one of his shift-mates could scoop it up with a shovel and dump it into a hopper. Hanson had wondered once or twice at the Factory, at Orange, at the State of York—at the incongruity of a society that must use unbelievably sophisticated machines and primitive hand-labor as integral parts of the same industrial process. Horses pulled the loaded ore-hoppers across Orange to the Docks, where a monster Utopian transport waited to carry it on the long journey to the ancient blast furnaces in Pitt, then skirting the Wall to the pockets of industry in the Chesapeake country, and then to the South. Horses and transports, autominers and shovels. The Utopian machines were used where they could be used, to do the magic work no army of ordinary men could do. Where they couldn't be used, where there were no machines anymore to be used for *that*, then the gap was filled in with hand-labor, with sweat and broken backs and sudden heart attacks. There were plenty of people after all.

And most of those people found nothing odd in the

arrangement. Hanson had once worked with the Utopian autominers, years ago, before factory politics and the enmity of Oristano the foreman had started him on the long road down to the Pit, and when he had first arrived at the Pit, at the rock bottom of his career with nowhere to go except death, he had remarked to old Relk in a mixture of bitterness and grim humor that it was too bad they couldn't scrape up a Goddamned Utopian machine to do the Goddamn shoveling. Relk had merely gaped blankly at him, unable to understand—Hanson might as well have spoken in a foreign language. Work was work; magic was magic; and that was that. Relk could see no incongruities, no connections between the two. He'd sniffed disapprovingly at Hanson and told him he wouldn't last long in the Pit.

But Hanson had worked like a hill demon his first few months in the Pit, and had finally replaced the old shift-leader, Ricciardi, after Ricciardi had died of a heart attack on the job. But that didn't cut any ice with Relk, "that didn't make no never mind" with him, as he would have said. No one lasted in the Pit as long as Relk, in the end. Others were transient; Relk was a permanent fixture.

Relk was staring at him now, his leather face wrinkling facilely into deep-worn lines of displeasure, so that he looked like a shriveled, thousand-year-old monkey with a bellyache. Hanson realized that he had been hesitating for a couple of minutes, leaning on his shovel and watching the gullet. He cursed himself wearily. As shift-leader, Hanson had the responsibility of pacing the work, setting the tempo and rhythm. He couldn't allow himself the luxury of daydreams—at least he wasn't supposed to. Angrily he scooped up another shovelful of coal, dumped it, came back for another. He forced himself back into the rhythm, concentrating on the movement of his body.

Relk snorted sourly and began shoveling again. Relk had never thought much of Hanson as a shift-leader. Hanson wasn't dedicated enough. Old Relk had worked the Pit for more than thirty-five years—his skin burned black, his skinny, knotted, cordwood body indestructible—and he'd seen at least ten shift-leaders come and go. None of them had been dedicated enough. Relk was dedicated—so dedicated his intelligence had long ago sunk down to the subhuman, which was why he'd never been chosen for shift-leader. He was totally absorbed by his job. He *was* his job, so much so that he no longer had any separate existence or identity. In many ways, then, he was the ideal citizen of Orange. He made Hanson's flesh crawl.

Hanson glanced surreptitiously down the line to see if anyone else had noticed his lapse. Gossard, next down beyond Relk, seemed oblivious to the world, grimly absorbed in his task. He was a little slower in the shoveling than the others—his motions faltered occasionally, the big blade wobbled every so often in his hands. His pale, globular body glistened slickly with sweat. The Pit was hard on Gossard. He was a good man, a friend, and a conscientious worker, but he was absurdly fat—the sickly, flabby fat of a glandular imbalance; few men got enough to eat in Orange to become fat in the traditional manner—and his weight told cruelly on him, especially in the summer. But he was trapped; he wasn't a fast enough worker to merit advancement out of the Pit, and the blacklist would deny him employment elsewhere if he should quit his job. It was hard enough to live on State salary; people without jobs often didn't live at all. If Gossard wanted his family to survive, he had to work here. It would kill him someday. The coal dust bothered him too, and he coughed constantly, great wracking coughs that set his fat to quivering like lard poured into a tub. Hanson wondered sometimes if the dust or a stroke would get Gossard first.

Beyond Gossard were the two workers with unpronounceable names who didn't speak Mercan very well: one burly, bland, and butter-colored; the other as dead-black as the coal, amazingly slight for Pit work, all whipcord muscle and jittery nervous energy—the track marks were vivid up and down his arms and legs, and some days his eyes were nothing but whites swimming with ruptured blood vessels, but as long as he did his work, nobody would complain until the day he finally collapsed. They were openly queer, sitting with sweaty arms wrapped around each other's necks during breaks and joking in their rapid, incomprehensible dialect, singing and fondling each other in the washroom, grinning obscenely at the other men. Nobody cared about that either, and some people openly envied them: women had been scarce in Orange for a number of years now. Hanson had privately named them Tic and Tac. Tic was now working with insane speed, but spastically, spilling coal, doing a jittery skipping dance dangerously close to the curb with every stroke, unable to remain still even for a second. Tac was slyly screwing off as usual, his face crafty as a cat's, but Hanson didn't feel like calling him on it so soon after his own dereliction.

He used his return swing for an excuse to glance to his left, where he had been wanting to look from the first, made hesitant by guilt and apprehension. They had put the New Man there this morning, just to Hanson's left, ostensibly so that Hanson could keep an eye on him. Hanson knew better. Hanson and Oristano the foreman had been deadly enemies for almost a decade and they understood each other with that special intense intimacy reserved for feuders and lovers. And Oristano's obscene shark grin this morning, as he introduced the New Man, had told the whole story. Oristano knew Hanson's pride, knew how it had been slowly battered down over the years until being the fastest, hardest worker in the Pit was the last thing Hanson had left to be proud of, knew how Hanson clung to that brag with the desperation of a drowning man.

And that it was no longer true.

The New Man was working with the dazzling, rock-steady rhythm he had displayed all morning, calm, fluid, and unrestrained, not even breathing hard. He was a huge bull of a man, a coffee-colored giant with kinky, flaming red hair. He was a solid barrel of muscle, carrying not an ounce of fat, and he was *young*. He was very young. Hanson had been a factory legend in his own time, but he was almost twenty years older than the New Man, and each day of those years sat like lead on his arms and legs, like a bar of iron across his shoulders. Hanson knew that he couldn't beat the New Man, not now, not after half a lifetime of killing labor—the New Man was young, magnificently fresh, fed by a hundred biological springs that had dried up in Hanson long ago.

He just couldn't keep up with him. That was bitter; that was very hard.

Maybe he never would have been able to match this monster, even in his prime.

That was unendurable.

The New Man had seen him daydreaming, like a toothless old fool, just when he would have been establishing his status over the younger man, when he should have been proving that he was still the hardest-working slug in the Pit. He had shamed himself before the New Man, he had disgraced his reputation at the very moment that he needed it the most. He was too old, his brain was going, he couldn't think anymore. Somebody should shoot him if he was getting that senile, roll him in a ditch, cover him up before he started to rot out in the open air. And the New Man was easily matching Hanson's quickest pace, with the unthinking grace and sureness of the young. In fact, it was obvious that he could go much faster if he wanted to but that he was restraining himself, he was deliberately holding himself back to Hanson's slower tempo.

The New Man was being *polite*.

And Hanson stopped thinking, except with his body.

Hanson began working faster, without volition—faster and faster, like a mechanical toy speeding up to a blur, wound too tight, out of control.

The New Man matched him easily, stroke for stroke.

Gossard faltered, dropped out. Tic and Tac kept up a little longer and then stopped, panting, watching in awe. Old Relk continued to work at his own personal speed, ignoring everybody, shaking his head at the decadence of the world.

The New Man had finally moved ahead of Hanson, opening up all the way. Hanson couldn't keep up. Already he had fallen three or four strokes behind—

To Hanson, it was as if the sun had melted and poured down over him in a cascade of scalding molten gold—he breathed it stabbingly into his lungs, it stripped the flesh from his bones, it broiled the marrow in the sockets, it piled up mountainously on his shoulders and crushed him with the weight of the sky. Slowly his legs buckled under the mass of the sky-mountain. He was talking to Becky now, and they were walking together through a high open meadow where the grass and trees were made all of ice, and flowers sprinkled like searfrost. But he couldn't keep up with her because the mountain was too heavy and he couldn't put it down. He tried to run after her, but the mountain crushed him like a giant's thumb and the icy ground softened to mud under his feet, and he sank into it under the mountain, floundering, sinking deeper and deeper. No matter what he had to

stop.

He did.

The shovel saved Hanson from actually falling. He leaned against it, legs rubbery, knees flexed, breath rasping in his throat. Oristano's face swam under his eyelids. It superimposed itself over the coal-mountain, the two things merging into an inhuman, undefeatable entity—a god of black malignancy. He opened his eyes. Slowly, his vision cleared. Planes of bloody shadow resolved into the New Man, who was staring at him with a worried, embarrassed expression. He caught Hanson's eye and smiled hesitantly—he didn't want to rub Hanson's face in his victory. He was still being very polite.

Gossard caught the tension in the air and went doggedly back to work, not wanting to watch Hanson's final humiliation. Tac made an obscure, fatalistic gesture with his fingertips; Tic stroked his shoulder, pursed wet lips—they started shoveling again. Relk looked around with an air of sly, senile vindication, made a muffled *hunh* sound, and turned away, muttering something about dedication to the coal pile as he dug his blade into it.

Hanson drew himself up. His arms and back throbbed as if they had been beaten with clubs and there was no strength in his legs; he wobbled in spite of his best efforts to brace himself. The New Man pretended not to notice. Hanson ran his tongue around his lips, tasted blood, swallowed it. Defeat slumped his spine, burned his brain to ash. He waited for some ashen thought to filter down through his new ash brain, but no thought came—it was as barren as the Moon. Sternly, he took control of his face and forced himself to smile back at the New Man. It wasn't really his fault; he was a good boy. Blame himself instead. Blame Oristano. Blame Time.

The New Man relaxed, visibly relieved—his smile broadened into a grin from which with all the best will in the world, it was impossible for him to keep a trace of satisfied triumph. This is his hour, Hanson thought, let him enjoy it. He was being good about it anyway, out of respect for Hanson's reputation. How very strange that was. When had living admiration become respect for a legend? How could the line have slipped up on him and past without his notice? Had he been that blind? Wasn't he still the same man he'd always been, below the old bones?

The New Man fished in his pocket and came up with a narc. He scratched the stick on his hip; the narc flared and then guttered to an orange ember-glow at its tip. A wisp of smoke curled up around his massive forearm like the ghost of a snake. The New Man offered the narc to Hanson: a friendly monster, smiling and huge, sweat runneling his broad face.

Hanson hesitated, studying the sweaty giant, and then took the narc. He put the horn-tipped end of the resin stick in his mouth and sipped deeply, holding a smoldering pine forest in his lungs. The New Man produced another narc. They stood smoking together while the sun baked them dry of sweat. Coal rustled unheeded around their feet.

"Hot sumbitch, a'n't it?" the New Man said.

"Ai," Hanson said, trying not to sound too much like a

dead man. Prodding himself: "A'ways is, this time of year. Freeze your ass off in winter though. A'ways one or the other, up here. You a'n't never going to be comfortable."

"Ai."

The New Man was staring out across the sweep of Orange: seas of hunched, dirty roofs, narrow alleys, smoke-belching chimneys, here and there the broken skeleton of a ruined Utopian building towering above the squalor, picked clean, naked and pathetic. "Can see a hell of a ways, though, up here," the New Man said enthusiastically. "Most all of the city I'll bet, near about."

"Ai, the whole Goddamn shitpile." He wouldn't turn his head to look at the Wall, though he was sharply aware of its presence. It beat against him like a hand of light, the knowledge of that golden, heartless thing.

Far as Hanson could tell from here, the Wall marched across the whole world and never came to an end. The Goddamned thing just never ended at all.

He blinked back sudden tears of rage and sorrow so great they squeezed his heart.

"Come on," he said, and punched the giant in the shoulder. And picked up his shovel.

And somehow he managed to keep working throughout the afternoon, although his mind was not there at all most of the time. His body seemed to manage well enough without it.

It was dark by the time the shift ended. Hanson gave the signal to quit work, and they shouldered their tools and shuffled single file along the curb to the lip of the Pit.

Oristano met them at the lip.

To Hanson, the foreman looked like a gross manikin sculpted from shadow, a hunched puddle of darkness that even starlight couldn't melt, merely glinting dully from teeth and eyes. He was backlit by the furnace glare that escaped around the iron doors behind him, and his bloated silhouette suddenly seemed to be that of a monster toad crouched in a smoldering sulfur swamp, waiting for weary flies to spiral hopelessly down within reach. Hanson could almost see the sticky, supple frog-tongue licking out, flickering impatiently down and around the foreman's waist. Then Oristano stepped forward, and the rough blob of his head split open to reveal an ugly, tooth-glinting grin. Oristano was big, half a head shorter than Hanson, but built broader and heavier. Hanson could remember him as a svelte bear of a man, covered with bristly black hair, clumsy but very powerful, and with a bear's sick, uncertain temper. Time and ease had added weight until now he was grossly fat—not the flabby stuff of Gossard's affliction, but tight-packed and well-muscled lard that made him look even more dangerous than he had in the past. Usually he was brusque with

Hanson, and the two spoke little to each other, making no attempt to hide their dislike. Tonight he greeted Hanson with boisterous good cheer and an exaggerated oily courtesy, asking Hanson in a loud voice if the New Man had worked out all right.

"Yes," Hanson answered quietly, "he works very well." The shovel felt incredibly heavy against his bruised shoulder. He bowed grudgingly under its weight. Alternate waves of hot and cold ran along his body, and a faint nausea returned. He could sense the New Man somewhere off to his right, embarrassed again, made uneasy by the sadistic malice in Oristano's voice and the weary, beaten hatred in Hanson's, aware that the two older men were acting out some ritual that he couldn't quite understand but in which he had played an integral part.

"He's a good worker, ai?" Oristano boomed.

"Yes," Hanson said.

Oristano grinned, another flash of crooked teeth. "Good, good." Flash again. "That's *good,* ai?"

Hanson nodded dully.

"*Ai.*" Oristano laughed, and waved a ponderous arm. Factory artisans rolled the fire door open—the sudden blast of hot light sent Oristano's shadow leaping out, swelling and elongating fantastically, washing over Hanson—and began to carry equipment out. Hanson's shift moved up from the curb, swirling around Hanson, and filed along the platform behind the lip to make room. The new shift waited by the fire doors as the artisans gingerly carried old spotlights out to position them along the curb. The line of artisans broke around Oristano: ants around a boulder. Neither man had moved. Oristano bulked like an ogre on the platform, gob-lin-grin glistening wetly. Hanson remained at the junction of curb and lip, shovel still slung across his shoulders, watch-ing wearily.

The artisans had clamped the spotlights to the curb at intervals, muzzles tilted up at an angle so that their glare wouldn't blind the shovelers, but would give enough light to work the Pit. Now they were stringing much-patched wires back along the underside of the curb, where they'd be out of the way of pivoting feet, and test-ing connections. The spotlights came on one by one, at low intensity: a herd of giant rheumy orange eyes—dinosaurs jostling down in the dark to drink. The nearest spot spilled shifting orange patterns across Han-son's knotted back, up and along the bulge of Oristano's naked belly. Then the spot came on at full strength, slic-ing a white column through jet. In the sudden glare, Han-son could see Oristano's face clearly for the first time that evening: heavy-jowled, eyes pinched shut with fat; lips absurdly small and delicate; a mashed, shattered nose laced with old white scars, hair peeking in tufts from the nostrils. The same beam illuminated the upper half of the pile and the ceaseless crawling of the coal.

All this, all these years, Hanson thought in numb horror, because I once broke Oristano's nose in a tavern brawl, in front of the men of the factory.

Nothing ever ended. Five minutes of his past had birthed all the rest of his life.

Hanson shifted the weight of the shovel and stepped up onto the lip. He walked past Oristano without looking at him and continued steadily on across the platform to the fire door. Oristano laughed again, an ugly clotted sound, and followed Hanson with his eyes, although he disdained to turn his head.

Fifteen years of shuffling around the giant factory, going from one section to another, from job to job, always falling lower, but always hanging on to one more hope—fifteen years, and now it was all over. He was finished. The New Man would be shift-leader tomorrow, although he didn't know it yet. Hanson would not come back. Oristano had known that he wouldn't. And without a job in Orange, barred from work by quitting the factory, Hanson was a dead man. He might as well lie down now and wait for the scavengers. It was all over with him.

Without saying a word, Hanson collected his shift and led them out through the fire doors, through the guts of the factory toward the washroom. He did not look back.

Behind him, Oristano smiled.

Hanson washed up slowly, working the tarnished brass pump, watching the hypnotically rhythmical spurts of rusty water fill the basin. His face was expressionless, and he ignored the other men in his shift. Relk, as usual, had merely changed into his civilian clothes and left, without bothering to wash, without bothering to say goodbye. Tic and Tac splashed noisily at the far basin, talking in a rapid stream of gutturals and fricatives. Gossard wallowed in armfuls of water, blowing like a whale. The New Man washed quietly, dressed, and then hesitated by Hanson's basin on the way out, feeling obliged to say something to the older man but afraid to speak. Hanson did not look up. After several moments, the New Man shrugged, shook his head, and left. Hanson continued to wash, stolidly, turning his arms over and over under the pump.

Moving with deliberation, he soaped the salty patches of dried sweat from his body, lifted the heavy ceramic basin, and poured the brackish water over his head, carefully pumped the basin full, and rinsed himself again. While he was doing this, Tic and Tac went out, each staring at him as they went by—Tac looking at him with morbid, insolent curiosity, as if he was examining a particularly interesting corpse, and Tic rolling his eyes in a quick sideways motion, as if he was afraid to look at Hanson directly, as if Hanson was the carrier of a disease so virulent it could be contracted by a glance. Hanson stood like a statue, holding the basin over his head, letting the water flatten his thinning black hair, cascade over his shoulders, pour in runnels down his legs. His eyes were fixed and unblinking. Tic and Tac hurried out, and didn't look back.

When the basin was empty, Hanson put it down and picked up a coarse towel, moving no more than necessary. He heard Gossard come up behind him, hesitating as the New Man had, a few steps away. Hanson rubbed himself down methodically, not turning around. Gossard shifted his weight uneasily from foot to foot, unconsciously sighing and massaging his stomach. Hanson could hear him breath: labored, wheezing, strangled by fat. He wouldn't last much longer, Hanson thought again. His heart, one day on the shift. Or a stroke. Or the dust. The thought made Hanson sad and almost pierced the wall that humiliation and the loss of status were building around him—he felt a momentary desire to talk to the fat man, to confess the shame and agony. To share his friendship while he's still alive, Hanson realized, in a wave of black fury. Before the job kills him. Like it will kill all of us eventually, one by one, until only old Relk is left. Or until we all become like him: dead, but still walking. Hanson snapped the towel viciously against his calf, relishing the sting, and began to rub himself down again.

Anger had rebuilt the walls of his shame, and he pointedly ignored Gossard, keeping his back turned. Why should one corpse talk to another? About what? Gossard cleared his throat obstreperously without eliciting any response, walked suddenly to the door, paused, and came slowly back.

"Carl?"

"Yes?" Hanson replied, without turning his head.

"Are you all right?"

Hanson's cheeks flamed. Half a lifetime leaped in his throat, tangled itself hopelessly in his tongue, refused to pass his lips. What he said was: "Yes."

"You're certain?"

"Yes."

Silence, Hanson standing motionless with the towel clutched in his hands like a snake, and then Gossard said, "Is there—" and Hanson said, "No," almost simultaneously.

Gossard tried again: "If there's anything I can do—"

"No."

Then, forcing himself to speak:

"No. Thank you, John, but no. Nothing."

Then:

"There is nothing that can be done."

There was a long silence and Hanson did not move at all. Gossard didn't speak again. After a while, he went away, closing the door gently behind him. The sound of his heavy footsteps dwindled into distance, was gone.

Hanson was alone.

The fading gurgle of water down sunken drains, the slow *drip-drip* of a faulty pump. The single carbon lamp flared and dimmed regularly with the beat of hidden dynamos, a brassy illumination washing across the stone walls and floor, ebbing from a beach of shadows. The air was heavy with old sweat. The room was full of ghosts.

Hanson was still for a moment longer, then, like a statue coming to life, he crushed the towel into a ball and hurled it viciously away, shuddering with disgust. He took a staggering step to a basin, braced his arms against it, and took three deep breaths, his backbone rising and falling with the effort. Gradually his breathing slowed. He became a statue again.

He had been sure he was going to be sick, but he couldn't: the sickness clogged somewhere in the very back of his throat, too deep ever to be regurgitated.

He pushed himself away from the basin, walked rapidly and violently to the center of the washroom, and stopped, looking around uncertainly, shaking his head, baffled. He started out again with great vigor, stopped after two steps, casting quick, frightened glances around him, seeing through the walls to the labyrinth of factory corridors, the maze of his life. He grimaced, rubbed his hands along his ribs, forced himself into motion, his steps dragging as if he were wading into quicksand, four steps, five, and he was halted again—stopped dead by inertia. He could feel the factory above him, below him, holding him in its belly, crushing down against his shoulders, anchoring his feet deep in its alien earth.

There was no place to go.

There was nothing to do.

There were no options left open to him.

Appalled, he allowed himself to drift back into the washroom, away from the door, along the row of basins, along the row of urinals. The stone under his feet was stained and porous, slightly damp—it felt like flesh. The air was delicately webbed with ancient piss, the light was spiky and hurtful against Hanson's eyes, his shadow drifted listlessly with him, across the grimy walls—the ghost of a ghost. He fetched up against the far wall, turned restlessly, and pushed into a wooden commode stall. The commode was old—stone-lipped, and earthen-breathed from the huge sump beneath the factory. It was now considered a luxury, and the use of it an incentive to work; the factory had been built in somewhat more prosperous times—the interlude between the Third Plague and the disastrous Campaign Against the South—when the State had been able to afford spending money and materials on such things, and when artisans sufficiently talented to build such a system were common enough to waste on nonessentials. Hanson had been raised with outhouses and nightjars at best, slit trenches or hand-scooped holes at worst, and still found the big stone commode alien and faintly menacing, in spite of years at the factory. He stared at it dumbly, as if expecting it to speak in a septic voice of decay.

Habit took over. Automatically, he sat down, tried to move his bowels. All the while, he watched himself, as if from a vantage point outside his body—one part of his mind was sardonically amused, one part was very afraid, and one part was murderously angry. The fearful part kept him going through the mundane actions of his normal life by rote, making him wash, dry himself, excrete—all rather desperately, as if by clinging to familiar routine he could negate and unmake the horrors of the day. The sardonic part was amused by the incongruity of trying to cling to normalcy when his life had just been blighted, destroyed, turned upside down, of carrying out the minutiae of life when he was dead. The angry part watched both others, and despised them both, and grew ever more angry at the conditions that had produced them—it knew nothing but hate.

There was an open, latticed window in the wall, giving a fine overview of the torchlit sprawl of nighttime Orange, but Hanson refused to look at it. He watched the wide lip of the window instead, the iron bars set in stone, the intricate networks of cracks and chips, the patterns of dirt and small pebbles, the mummified bodies of flies—watched them until they had no meaning to him anymore, until they were completely alien to him, incomprehensible, and then he watched nothing at all, just as intently although his eyes were no longer focused. The stone underneath his buttocks was cold, and the night wind through the window was damp on his naked body. Instinctively, he brought his knees closer to his chin, wrapped his arms around his legs. He sat alone and naked in the cold belly of the factory, surrounded by yards of chill stone and the even colder ruins of his life, rocking back and forth, hugging his knees. This was the time to cry—he knew it, wanted to, longed for the release crying would bring. But the tears would not come. They hung, burning, somewhere behind his eyes, but they would not fall. Tears were for the living, not the dead.

And he could not move his bowels, although his stomach ached. He was completely dead now, dry, sterile, shriveled, his blood curdled in his veins, his seed killed in the sack, his bodily openings sewed tightly shut. He moved a hand through the thick tangle of hair on his chest—his skin was slick and cold as rock and he was unable to feel his heartbeat—across his ribs, along his huge arms, his massive, corded legs. There was a roll of fat beginning at his waist, in spite of work, in spite of his poor diet. The muscles were beginning to sag slightly on the undersides of his arms and thighs, and veins stood out on his legs as if they were done in relief. He was losing his hair and his skin was starting to crack and yellow, like sunbaked mud. He was getting old. And there was a dull pain in his stomach, always present, although sometimes it would stir sluggishly, like a blunt-headed beast inside him that wanted to get out. The Crab was in there—he had suspected it for months, known it for weeks, finally admitted it to himself. He had seen the Crab take his uncle, his cousin, his brother's wife, his friend Matthew, and now it was going to take him. It would take him within the year.

And what had his life been *for*?

Hanson stopped rocking. He sat very still, listening to the world wind down, listening to his body decay. Now it was as if his mind was a blinking light, first flashing red, then black. When it flashed black he would huddle freezing and paralyzed, immobilized by despair and futility, unable to move, unable to think. When it flashed red, he regained the ability to move, but only in one direction; to think, but only one thought—his frozen limbs thawed in the furnace of rage, but the furnace had been stoked for only one purpose. The light of his mind flashed black and red, red and black, and each time the red light remained on a little longer than the black, and longer, and longer still, like a spun coin wobbling toward collapse, until finally the black light vanished completely and the red light blazed as steady and smoky as blood.

Hanson got to his feet, pushed out of the commode stall—the wooden door boomed with hollow finality in the silence, in the empty room.

Moving quickly and surely, he dressed, laced on his boots, and left the washroom. There was no hesitation in him now: he was all economy and efficiency, his actions flowing together as smoothly as quicksilver as he threaded the factory corridors. He walked with a steady, springy stride, full of authority and self-assurance, cruising through the building like a big, dark clipper ship under full sail. There were few people about at this time of night, and none of those he encountered thought to question him, or even paid any attention to him at all—he too obviously knew where he was going and why. His expression was calm and absorbed; only a close look would have revealed the strain in that face, the tiny lines around the eyes, the bloodless tension of his lips.

He crossed half the width of the giant building to a little-used stairway, ascended two levels, went out a storeroom window, across a low roof, up a metal ladder in the inky darkness, in another window—squeezing awkwardly between the two boards that haphazardly sealed it—up one more level by another dusty back stairway, along a deserted corridor, and so arrived back at the shift room unseen. He knew the rounds of all the watchmen and State Inspectors perfectly, by the second and by the inch, and he had dodged three of them by this roundabout route, passing successfully through their territories just before or just after they did: the watchmen would swear that no one could have passed them unobserved, and that might help to cloud matters a little, or so the rational layer of his mind hoped, although he was too far gone now to worry much about consequences—he had acted mostly out of an animal instinct that had told him not to let himself be seen, to avoid other men because he was, in this moment, alien to them.

The shift room was empty, echoing and too bright under the carbon lamps. The big metal lockers looked like rows of drab tombstones, light winking coldly and malevolently from their polished faces. Hanson crossed the room unhurriedly and used one of his keys to open a locker. He took out a shovel, carefully doctored the supply sheet to make it appear that the shovel had been issued to one of the men now on shift, and closed the locker up again. Then he walked to a door half hidden by the row of lockers, opened it with another key, stepped briskly inside, and locked it behind him.

This was a big supply room, seldom in use: dark, smothering, full of the slumbering, shrouded shapes of crates and barrels, steeped through with pungent, unidentifiable stinks. The only light came from far on the other side of the room, very dim and pale, as if it was leaking in from another world.

Hanson made his way slowly through this dusty tangle, oozing around the nearly invisible crates with preternatural ease, making no sound. In the darkness, he appeared less human, more feral: thicker and broader, bulkier, goblin-shaped and glitter-eyed, too sure and cat-footed for a man. He held the heavy, iron-bladed shovel like a twig, like a fey child with a switch.

A rectangle of smoky light: a door.

Hanson settled down to wait, squatting on his hams behind a tall packing crate. He knew Oristano's schedule as well as he knew every other detail of factory routine, knew it in both the overt and covert details, as the foreman was a creature of long-established habit in all things. The second night crew had gone on shift about a half hour before; in an hour Oristano would go on an inspection tour of those sections under his authority, poking and prying and making the workers uncomfortable, as he was hired to do. In the meanwhile, he would be in there fucking fat Emily, the tumorous whore from the Bog, on the cot in his office. In about a half hour, Oristano would finish fucking fat Emily, they would share the obligatory cigarette, and he would let her out the other door—she had another regular appointment on the hour, with Oristano's immediate superior. Then Oristano would cook a C and M speedball—crystal cocaine and morphine—over a small brazier, bang himself with it, and settle down to wait for the rush, and to drink enough corn whisky to ensure that he was in a sufficiently evil mood for his tour. After the whore left, he would be alone in his office for a half to three-quarters of an hour: no one would dare disturb him then, no matter what. Everyone knew better.

A muffled jumble of sound: voices.

Oristano would be alone.

A shrill laugh, silence, the sound of bedsprings.

Hanson hefted the shovel in his hands.

The dust tickled his nose and tiny spiders scampered across his arms, across his face, like the touch of gentle, invisible fingers. They were the shy, albino spiders that inhabit dusty corners in dark buildings and spin gossamer out of disuse—they never saw the sun. They used Hanson for a highway, washing over him in a waterfall of velvet feet while he sat in the shadows and listened to the factory: the massive, deep-throated beat of pistons far below reechoed through every joint and seam of the building, conducted through cement and wood, shaking the room, shaking his blood, shaking the teeth in his head, shaking the brain inside his skull, boom*doom*, boom*doom,* boom*doom,* boom*doom,* until he was somehow on his feet, shaking uncontrollably, convulsively squeezing wood to keep it in his hands, shaking, being shaken, jarred, jostled, jolted, being frog-marched toward the door in a lurching stiff-legged stride, trying to remember that he had to wait, *wait,* although it was hard to remember what he had to wait for. He stopped just outside the door, fingertips resting on the wood, wondering why it didn't explode inward under the force of the pressure behind him, why it didn't shatter and fly to flinders, as he was shaken by the surge of the world that wrenched his bones out of his body, boom*doom,* boom*doom.*

Inside, voices again, louder now, another laugh, footsteps going away, the slamming of another and more distant door, a single set of heavy footsteps returning.

Suddenly smooth as silk and steady as skin, as if he had instantly shifted into a different gear, Hanson reached out and opened the door.

The room was dingy and cluttered: a table, two chairs, a cot, a washbasin, a cabinet. Oristano's broad back was toward the door—he had not heard it open. He was rummaging in the cabinet, taking out a hypodermic needle and a rusty spoon. An ancient revolver, symbol of his position and authority, sat in its holster on the table, three feet away.

Now, said Hanson's blood, *while his back is turned.* But

instead he heard his own voice, as if from a great distance, speaking Oristano's name aloud, as a rock might speak, or ice.

Oristano knew death when he heard it. Without bothering to look around, he whirled and snatched for the table. His shadow swung and scurried like a crab behind him. He was awesomely fast for a man of his bulk. He had the gun in his hand and had brought it halfway around to bear before Hanson's shovel, swung in a short horizontal arc of immense force, crushed his head.

The force of the blow spun Oristano in a misty explosion of blood and brains, and hurled him heavily against the table, which splintered and collapsed. The table and Oristano went down together, in a tangle.

Except for the meaty slap of the shovel and the crack of breaking wood, there had been no sound.

The hypodermic needle teetered on the edge of the cabinet, then toppled very slowly to the floor. It shattered with a tiny glass cry, like the breaking of a fragile dream.

Hanson stood motionless, holding the shovel. His arms tingled from impact, and a splinter had dug into his palm. The blow had nearly decapitated Oristano, and the body, in falling, had sprayed blood across half the room, the cot, the ceiling. Most of the spray had missed Hanson, but his face had been lightly, almost delicately, dusted with a fine sprinkling of droplets, as if he was a child playing at measles with garish red paint. He took one hand off the shovel and absently wiped at his eyes with his knuckles, smearing the blood. He continued to wipe at it, grinding it into his skin.

He looked down at Oristano's body. With his killing blow, with the first touch of impact, the red light in Hanson's mind had instantly gone out, leaving him with no purpose or plan, drowned in the paralytic black light of despair. Now he was like a man waking, stupid and desolate, from a particularly evil dream—or else like a man swimming down from the border of dream into another, even more troubled sleep, unable to wake although he knows that he should. The room around him seemed blurred and vague, his memory of the past hour even more vague; he remembered his actions as if another man had done them while he watched, only dimly able to guess at that man's motives and feelings. Oristano's bloated corpse filled him with surprise and horror. He felt no emotional responsibility for it as yet, no sense of it being a child of his hands, but it seemed so charged with *outré* significance, so remarkable and unnatural an object in itself, that it flooded him with superstitious dread: he could imagine the shattered, faceless man rising, confronting him, embracing him with cold arms, smothering him. Absorbing him tracelessly into its bulk.

And now there was a sickness starting deep inside, a

spreading numbness that drove the room even further away. He shook his head stupidly, baffled as a bull. He couldn't wake up. The room spitefully refused to change, to alter—it remained starkly and harshly the same, and he mired in the middle of it with murder in his hand and death all around. And now there was a noise, a scrape of wood on wood. Through numbing waves of nausea, he looked up.

Tac stood in the doorway: face bland as butter, eyes shrewd and malefic.

There was his doom, Hanson realized with tranced calm and logic. Tac was poised for flight, holding the door ready to slam after him; he was the entire length of the room away, on the other side of Oristano's body; from that other door the main entrance of the shift room was only six paces distant, down a short corridor—even if Hanson should try to attack him, all Tac would have to do was slam the door and run out into the shift room, shouting for help. Long before Hanson could hope to catch up to him and silence him—if Hanson could get his numb, leaden body to move at all—Tac would have the place boiling with workmen, watchmen, State Inspectors. Escape would be impossible—they would run him down in seconds, subdue him, take him away. Then the gallows, the block, a bullet in the head, maybe a public stoning or the stake since this had been a dull season in Orange. No way out. No way to stop Tac, no way to talk him into silence. Tac would surely get a big promotion for turning Hanson in, and Hanson had nothing to bribe him with anywhere near the value. And to appeal to the charity of that sly, cruel creature would be like entreating fire not to burn.

All this in a second, Tac looming in the doorway, Hanson staring hopelessly at him across the tilted landscape of Oristano's corpse. Then, before either man had a chance to move, Tac's face suddenly changed: his slitted eyes widened enormously, huge with surprise; his cheeks puffed, his mouth gaped impossibly—all his broad face, all his stubby body seemed to swell, blowing up like a balloon, expanding like a pufferfish straining at the limits of his skin until it seemed certain he would explode and splatter. And then Tac went limp—ponderously he fell, first to his knees, then forward to his face, almost lazily, shouldering into death as a man settles into a warm and restful bed.

Gossard stepped into the room, behind Tac. There was a knife in his hand, and the blade steamed with new blood.

2

ORANGE IS A SPRAWLING, ugly town, situated a few miles west of the historic site of Old Orange, something to the north of what was once St. Cloud. It is made mostly of wood and fired clay, sunbaked mud, some sections of fine brick and iron put up during the fleeting prosperous decade of the Great Restoration when York was carving an empire out of the checkerboarded squabble of the northwest, before the fortunes of the State began to decline. It contains a large proportion of Utopian buildings, although few are completely standing, and only a very few are in anything resembling usable condition. It is primarily a trading town, serving as a funnel and middleman for the traffic between the Stabilities of Portland, Pitt, and the South, all of the trade that follows the main routes skirting the Wall of the City of God. It also contains what passes today for heavy industry, and is well-known for leather tanning and textiles. It is the third-largest city in York, and, since the destruction of Worcester, the most eastern of all the really big towns in the Human Domain, south of Portland.

Tonight, it simmered.

Deep in a parched, brutal summer, the city stewed and steamed like sluggish porridge over a flame. Heat poured in from the west, as though tilted from a giant's ladle, filled the city to the brim, and then hardened—like wax, like amber, catching and preserving everything within the fierce dry ocean of itself.

In Orange, all motion had stopped. The life of the city sank to a torpid minimum, the occasional patient twitching of a toad buried in mud at the bottom of a riverbed, hiding from the sun. People huddled in their shanty homes, stunned by heat, stacked like corpses in the smothering dark. There was no wind. Torches burned without wavering, their smoke stretching straight up, as if they were lines attached to a hook in heaven. Heat swallowed sound like a mountain of feathers, damping it, sopping it up. Even the air itself seemed to have been sucked away, molecule by molecule, and replaced with a clear liquid glass that one could somehow breathe without ever quite suffocating completely, but which never afforded any comfort or relief.

To Hanson, sitting on top of an ancient Utopian freight transport crawling through Orange from the Docks toward South Gate, it seemed as if the hush and suspension of the night were aimed at him, as if the whole city were holding its breath in horror at what he had done. Or perhaps the city was gathering that breath for a great shout, a scream, the hush breaking in an instant and boiling with sudden faceless pursuit, the pointed finger, *there* he is, the contaminated one, the fugitive, the killer, *there,* and the horny, impersonal hands pulling him down, pulling him under, rending his bones apart in a single ecstatic explosion of blood . . . Hanson shifted his feet on the deckplates, bracing himself better against the rolling of the massive old machine. There was no pursuit yet. The shabby buildings of the Blackstone district watched him with disinterest, drooping lids of windows, slack-gaped mouths of doors, leaning against each other in weariness and defeat—they had seen too much, known too much; they didn't care about Hanson, or his crime.

The sweltering torpor of Orange suited Hanson's mood tonight—still half dazed, drained, and shaken by the violence of his passion at the factory, unable to keep up with a bewilderingly fast tumble of events. Like a graveyard, silent Orange was both disconcerting and peaceful, radiating an inevitable certainty of death that was oddly comforting. The city might have been an open grave, yawning dumbly at the stars, weighted down with the dead but not yet filled in with raw earth. In many ways it was just that—an open grave; always had been, always would be, until the last of its scurvy inhabitants succumbed to disease, hunger, war, murder. And then would someone, something, come along to kick the dirt down over man?

They had come up from the Docks without seeing anyone at all—unusual, since the magic, lumbering passage of a Utopian machine was a minor event, and normally the streets would have suddenly swirled with people at their approach, certainly hordes of grimy children, all hoping for a moment's release from the monotony and brutality of their lives. But the killing heat had won out over curiosity, over magic. Industry Hill had been deserted when they skirted around its base, as it had been earlier when Hanson had descended from the factory in the dazed clamor of his own blood. Even the State Inspectors who usually swarmed the Hill to guard against sneak thieves were hiding inside from the weather; but then, so too were the sneak thieves. As they rumbled through the edges of Prospect Terrace, Hanson had seen a drunk pissing contentedly on the fine stone house of a prosperous wool merchant—a harbinger of the slums, and a bellwether of the night: no SIs around to stop him, as he would usually have been intercepted long before reaching the Swank. Now, as they turned downhill toward the center of Blackstone and the Bog, and as the neighborhood crumbled and deteriorated appallingly, he saw people in the streets for the first time: sullen, sluggish crowds who were out on the street because they lived there, in the street; because they had nowhere else to go.

Behind him, the State Factory shouldered against darkness, an island of brazen light, a mountain of iron—an open flame flickered red from its top, like a tongue. Lesser industries, lesser buildings clustered around its massive flanks: attendants to the Lord of Hell. It was a sight he had seen every evening for fifteen years, but now it made him uneasy and afraid, as if the factory was watching him with hungry furnace eyes, as if it would stride monstrously after him on legs made of stone and shadow, a demon cat after a mouse. It would have Oristano's face.

Murderer, he thought, trying it on for size.

In spite of himself, he turned his head every few seconds while they crawled down the slope to the Bog, keeping an eye on the factory until it was swallowed by a jumble of low roofs, as Industry Hill sank below the outskirts of Blackstone.

Gossard had saved him.

The feral half of Hanson's mind, the killer that had taken control to hunt Oristano, had thought itself clever—dodging the watchmen and State Inspectors, stalking its prey, waiting in ambush. But Tac had been much smarter than Hanson. He had sensed Hanson's anguish and turmoil, figured out what Hanson would do before Hanson himself knew, extrapolated the consequences and decided how best to turn them to his financial advantage; laying an ambush of his own to catch Hanson murdering Oristano. And Gossard had been smarter than Tac. Gossard had seen Tac skulking near the washroom, and had figured the whole tangle out in one intuitive, empathetic flash: what Hanson was doomed to do, what Tac's avarice would drive him to do in response, and what he himself must do to save his friend's life. And he had, setting a counter-ambush to silence Tac before he could betray Hanson.

In the whole web of intrigue, only Hanson had been stupid.

Passion had driven him to a blind crime, poorly conceived, clumsily executed—*stupid*. Only luck had saved him, for the moment, from the consequences of the act. And he was still stupid—now he was *fleeing* stupidly, blindly, stumblingly, with no plan, no purpose, no destination. If not for Gossard, Hanson told himself bitterly, he would probably still be standing in Oristano's office like a heatstruck ox, waiting dumbly for the SIs to come and collect him. It had been Gossard who had gotten him going again, who had jolted him a little out of his daze, who had set the mechanism of escape in motion.

It had been Gossard who had locked the doors to Oristano's office from the outside and, leading Hanson by the elbow like a sleepwalker, helped him dodge the watchmen and make his way safely outside the factory. And it was also Gossard who destroyed the fantasy of Hanson concealing his guilt: everyone in the factory knew of the vendetta between Hanson and Oristano, and the moment Oristano was found dead, everyone would know who had killed him. The factory SIs wouldn't even bother to carry out an investigation. They'd know who to arrest.

"Get out of Orange tonight," Gossard had said. "Get as far away as you can before morning, and keep on going. They'll put their hands on you if you're anywhere in the city, but if you skip entirely, go up the country, they won't look for you very far. Oristano wasn't *that* important. But get out quick. And don't tell anybody where you're going—" And he'd looked up at Hanson out of his sick, fat face, more strained and pale than ever with the heat. Hanson had realized, in one of those flashes of intuition that approach prophecy, that Gossard didn't have much longer to live, that his health had deteriorated too far to stand the summer ahead, that Gossard probably knew it, that certainly both of them were aware they'd never see each other again, and found nothing in his vocabulary adequate to that kind of goodbye. So they'd stared at each other for a long, awkward moment until Hanson finally blurted "Come with me," knowing as soon as he said it that Gossard would never desert his family and could never get them safely out of Orange, that Gossard would play out his role till he dropped, knowing what would happen but unable to get off the wheel. Gossard had merely shaken his head, said "Luck," and lumbered back into the factory, shutting the service door behind him, committing Hanson to the night.

With luck, Hanson had until the morning, maybe until noon, to get out of Orange. When Oristano missed tonight's inspection tours, it would be assumed that he had taken too much dope, or drank too much whisky, and was sleeping it off in his office behind locked doors. It had happened before; nobody would think too much of it, nobody would dare try to wake him up. Probably nobody would begin to wonder until sometime tomorrow. Then they would try to wake Oristano by knocking, try again, and eventually someone would have the guts to go find a master key and investigate. Maybe noon, maybe not.

And where was he supposed to *go*?

Nowhere on foot, that had been certain. Even dazed, he retained that much logic. The nearest village was Garfield, thirty miles away, and that hardly more than an SI garrison to maintain an old stone bridge over the Passaic. Too far, in one sense, over dangerous ground, alone.

Not far *enough,* quick enough, in another sense. It was unlikely they'd bother to search that far afield for him, but if they did he'd be finished: only one usable road to Garfield, only two roads out of Garfield north, and more than thirty miles to the next village—he could be easily run down by mounted men, who just might check Garfield because it was the obvious place for a fugitive afoot to go. And once he started out on foot, he'd stay on foot. Orange was the only place within a hundred miles where he might be able to find an alternative to walking.

And so he'd gone to the Docks, and his luck had held. There had been four caravans loading up at the land-docks, in spite of the heat and the late hour—the Docks were the deep-beating heart of the city's commerce, of its life, and they never shut down. Three of the caravans were hauled by the clumsy, potbellied steam-tractors, all pig iron and pistons, boisterous and bellowing. The fourth was headed by a sleek Utopian transport, an untarnishable, indefatigable giant of high steel, twelve feet tall by thirty feet long, more than four hundred years old and still running as smoothly and perfectly as an engineer's dream, running continuously for all of those four centuries without need of refueling or repair—magic. It had been built long before the creation of the ancient and venerable Government of the State of York, and it would probably be around long after the State had guttered and died, maybe even after there were any men left in the dwindling world to run her. But now, in the haunted interregnum of Earth, she was captained by Johann Willis and headed north this trip, to the Stabilities of Portland. And Johann Willis was an acquaintance of Hanson's. Not a close friend, but an acquaintance, and an occasional drinking companion—and the uncle of Hanson's dead wife, Hanson's Becky, down and dead in the flinty soil of York for more than four years. That was a blood-bond between them. Maybe it would be enough.

They reached the bottom of the slope and turned right, paralleling the open, ceramic-lined sewage trench that ran down the middle of Canal Street. The transport lurched as the road changed from worn cobblestone to thigh-deep mud, then its massive treads found traction and it steadied—the clumsy steam-tractors sometimes foundered in the rutted morasses that passed for streets in this section of summer Orange, but the ancient transport was nearly unstoppable. It wallowed ponderously along Canal Street, throwing a wake of mud on either side. Dense clouds of mosquitos and stinging black flies rose up out of the mire at the transport's approach, and settled again, swirling and buzzing angrily, when it had passed. Hanson swore irritably and slapped at his face; almost immediately, he was bitten again, on the back of his hand and then on the neck. Brigault, the Mate, grinned at Hanson from his position on the broad spine of the transport—he was wearing a hood of fine-meshed netting, and heavy black leather gloves in spite of the heat. "A bitch, a'n't it?" Brigault shouted jovially over the pounding of the engines. "But you gots to get flies, *ai*? The whole place is made out of shit!" The Mate grinned at Hanson again, enormously, revealing a mouth crowded with crooked, broken snaggleteeth. Brigault seemed to be having a fine time. And another two flies bit Hanson.

Dispiritedly, Hanson pulled his head as far into his coat as he could, like a turtle. It was, if possible, even hotter here than it had been on the Hill, and the stench alone was almost enough to knock a man down and kill him: offal, carrion, endless middens of hundred-year-old garbage, raw industrial sewage running through the Ditch, rank and sulfurous clouds of chemical smoke drifting downwind from the factories on Industry Hill. This was the center of the Bog, the Valley, the Sink, whichever you wanted to call it—the cancerous, ulcerated underbelly of Orange, the nadir of a city where even the rich had never risen too very far above subsistence. Rickety, narrow buildings lined Canal Street by the hundreds, rearing precariously up on either side of the open sewage trench, the Ditch, like rheumy, arthritic animals who had come down to drink of the foul water before they died. Some of these hovels were nine or ten stories high, and none of them were wider across the base than the width of a single room. They were made of mismatched wooden beams, bricks, paving-stones, all stuck together with clay and mud and mortar any way they would hold—some of them were so unsteady that they had to be propped up with poles braced in the ground, and all of them would sway and totter sickeningly in any kind of a wind. There was seldom even a handsbreadth of space between one structure and another, and many actually did lean against their neighbors, so that if a building did finally collapse, it usually took two or three others with it. No matter: a horde of homeless people and "contractors" would swarm through the rubble, strip—and sometimes eat—the corpses, and salvage what building materials they could. Within a few weeks, new buildings would have been raised under the brutal direction of the "contractors," cannibalized from the debris of the fallen, and people would be bribing and murdering with total ruthlessness to obtain the privilege of inhabiting them. This had been going on for hundreds of years, and it was doubtful that any building in the Bog had survived intact; they all toppled down into junk and were reassembled out of that same junk, over and over again, like shabby phoenixes. Every decade or so, a fire would rip through the Bog and destroy huge swaths of it, followed inevitably by Plague, a year or two later. But the Bog was indestructible—it would eat a little deeper into Blackstone, transforming the swallowed sections into the Bog; building materials would be found somewhere, somehow, and the hovels would rise again. And soon everything would be just about the same as it had ever been.

This had been my life, Hanson thought numbly, staring into the depths of the leprous warrens. A little bit better, perhaps, but not much. Blackstone instead of the Bog. Malnutrition instead of outright starvation, lingering sickness instead of immediate death. At least a pretense of a roof over his head, although some winters he'd wondered if it could be much colder even out on the street. A difference only in degree, not in kind. That was what he had bought with his youth, with his life. With Becky. And always the underlying threat of the Bog, of a fall into the Bog. Inevitable, waiting for all of them when they could no longer work hard enough to keep themselves out of it. In the end, all roads led downhill to it, to the Bog.

There was a fresh corpse floating in the Ditch, and he watched it bob and swirl with the current until, just before it was too far behind to see, two men with a travois fished it out of the water.

Ahead, the crowds became denser. The transport slowed, slowed again, almost—but not quite—coming to a stop. It inched through the muck, ponderous and irresistible. The crowd parted reluctantly around it—sometimes a man would wait until the giant treads were almost touching him before his courage broke and he foundered out of the way, slipping, falling, rolling. And then he would climb up out of the mud—plastered and stinking with it, rubbing it out of his eyes—and spit at the transport, or shake his fist. Hanson could see mouths moving in the crowd, teeth bared, men grinning with hate; he could hear shouts and obscenities, rising thinly above the sound of the engine. Someone threw a clot of mud that spattered against the deckplates; another. These were the dregs of the Bog: lobos, offenders whom even the casual butcher that was State justice found too unimportant to kill; homeless and unregistered children; junkies; gene-scrambled sports; decrepit whores; the infirm, the aged, the blacklisted—all those who couldn't work, or were not allowed to. They lived like wild dogs, on garbage, on what they could steal, on each other. They slept in the street, on the steps of the shanty homes of the more fortunate poor, in alcoves, under bridges. By the thousands. And every winter they died, by the thousands. And every spring there was another thousand, or two, to replace them—filtering down, no longer able to hold even a place in the middle terrace of Bog society. Their despair was a tangible pressure, black as coal; the heat crushed it into hate, diamond-bright, diamond-hard hate, tight and dangerous, gave it something to work on. There was a solid wall of men a few yards in front of the transport, and they did not look like they were going to move. Some of them were holding knives, some clubs, some torches, and their faces made the flesh crawl around Hanson's stomach and groin. Suppose one of them had a bow, or a javelin, or a scorpion—

Up in the cab, Johann Willis hit the whistle. The giant bellow of it slammed the high building walls on either side of the road and washed back, filling the world. The faces of the crowd went slack, shattered by sound, and then firmed up again when reason returned. But they had been shaken. They clutched their weapons uneasily and blinked around them, as the thunder died in grumbling echoes from the street. Willis hit the whistle again. The crowd was ready for it this time, but they still flinched, and when their faces set themselves up again, a little determination had gone out of them. The whistle blasted twice more. Buffeted, the rickety shanty buildings swayed and trembled, and a board crosswalk connecting two of them was jolted loose: it fell, sending an onlooker who had been lounging on it hurtling twenty feet down into the mud. Incongruously, someone in the crowd laughed. And instantly, as if that was his cue, Brigault was on his feet and at the edge of the deck, leaning out, bracing himself against a stanchion. He had pushed the netting back from his face, and his revolver was in his hand. "*Move* your asses!" Brigault screamed. "*Move 'em!*" He was grinning ferociously at the crowd; his eyes flickered back and forth, very fast, and the revolver moved with his gaze, so that first one man, then another found himself staring straight into the gun's ugly muzzle. Willis had poked his head up above the three-quarter shield of the cab—he said nothing, but he raised an ancient repeating rifle and slowly brought it down so that it was braced against his left forearm. Brigault shouted again. When the crowd did not move, he seemed to be amused. His grin softened into a smile that was even more frightening. "Move, Goddamn you," he said, not at all loudly, almost with affection. "*Move.*" There was something infinitely hard in his voice, riding it like a carrier beam, and the crowd flinched at the sound of it. Hesitantly, they moved—men stepping back, then changing their minds and stepping forward, then stepping back again. Willis caught the ripple of movement; he must have made some imperceptible signal, because the whistle screamed again at that moment, longer and louder than before. At once, the crowd broke. Grudgingly, they flowed aside, like some heavy, sluggish liquid, and let the transport through. Most of them didn't look up as it passed; they studied their feet and slogged wearily away through the mud. Willis ducked back down into the cab. In a moment, the transport was picking up speed once more. Its whistle hooted again and again, scornful in victory.

Brigault came walking back along the spine, rolling effortlessly with the motion of the vehicle. He sat down next to Hanson and patted the revolver in its holster. "No sweat," he said, "no problem." He grinned at Hanson. "Sometimes we gots to really *shoot* a couple, when they gets, you know, real stubborn. Mule-headed. They gets real mule-headed, in the hot weather." He spat, casually. "Or just run them right over. *Ai*, that's even better, that works real good. But they *a'ways* move. Eventu'ly. *Oh* yes." And he flipped the netting back down over his face with his thumb, and settled back against another stanchion. He looked very comfortable. He didn't move or speak again for a long while, and he might almost have been asleep. But his eyes glittered through the mesh, and they missed nothing.

Hanson tried several words on his tongue, but none of them worked.

He sat in prudent silence, and swatted blackflies.

In another half hour, the transport had crawled through South Gate, and was beginning to pull clear of Orange. There wasn't too much in the way of suburbs: one or two quarries, a few truck farms, some night-shrouded gypsy trading camps, a large garrison of the standing Army of York—carefully not allowed *inside* the city itself since the last "reorganization"/palace revolution/civil war—a deserted roadside shrine, and then, after a long stretch of nothing, a final SI post commanding a crossroads. No outlying villas, or estates, or summer homes, or middle-class residential areas, as there might have been in another age. It was dangerous to live outside the city walls, and few did, except for the gypsies and free-traders who were themselves too feral to be afraid, and the armed troops who were there to keep marauders away from the city—and the marauders, of course.

And then Orange was gone, completely, and the night closed in, black and smothering. The transport's headlight, at medium intensity, pushed the night about fifty yards away in front, but it closed down behind them even more dark and menacing, as if it resented the intrusion of the light. Brigault sent the other two crewmen walking down the train to hang lanterns at the couplings, and one at the tail. The transport was pulling a train load of eight cars this trip, and the lanterns helped the driver judge the position of that long, awkward tail accurately enough to get around curves without jackknifing it. The wood-and-iron freight cars were clumsy, ponderous things, but the transport pulled them easily, and could have pulled four times their number if the poor condition of the roads did not disallow it. To compensate, the cars were built deep and filled to overflowing—their loads barely contained by the tarpaulins lashed down taut over every car—and the cargo hold of the transport itself, under Hanson's feet, was stuffed full of the smallest and most valuable items. In spite of the weight, the transport moved swiftly through the darkness, sure and graceful, and Hanson was once again filled with rueful awe at the skill of the Utopian artisans. It was easy to understand the attitude of people like Relk; indeed, of most people—Hanson knew, intellectually, that the transport was "merely" a product of superior engineering, but it still seemed like magic to him, and he responded to it in that way, emotionally. The gap between those ancient people and himself was too great; so much had been lost and forgotten . . .

They were running through a stretch of scrub forest that alternated with sand and clay barrens. It was desolate, forlorn country, especially by starlight on a moonless night. They followed a curve around the shoulder of a small hill; there was a light way up the hill, just below the crest, the lit window of a building shrouded by trees. It shone high and lonely, a cold star riding above the earth, below the sky. Then the road dipped, and it was gone. Hanson realized that he would never know what the building was, or who lived there, or why, or if someone had been at that window, listening to the transport breathe mournfully by in the night, watching the lanterns bob like a string of blurred red jewels, perhaps wondering what eyes rode the train and were looking invisibly back up. The thought made Hanson sad. Life was like that—you rushed by others in the dark without knowing they were there, you left them behind; each minute buried a thousand possibilities, each turning killed a thousand alternate lives, and you had to say farewell constantly to people you would never meet. And still you rushed on. Hanson became aware that Brigault was watching him closely, although he could no longer see the Mate's eyes. He forced himself to relax, to sink back down against the deckplates. He was trembling. Nothing then but night and motion, until they pulled abreast of another SI outpost, a big half-timbered building surrounded by a tall earthwork wall, ablaze with torches, Bloomfield Station. A potbellied SI in his shirtsleeves, a half-eaten chicken drumstick in one hand, stood by the side of the road and waved them on. An embankment ahead, tall and *long*, diagonally across their path. And a ramp.

The transport had been heading east, more or less. Now it flowed up the ramp, turned left, and began to crawl north. This was an ancient highway, unbelievably huge in comparison to modern roads—a half-dozen transports could have traveled it abreast without crowding each other, and it stretched on endlessly ahead, dead black, like a frozen river made out of the night-fabric itself. The transport picked up speed. On such a good surface, Willis was certain to open it all the way up; he would be unable to for seven-eighths of the trip. They rocked and clicked along at a terrifying clip, but even Hanson knew that this was the safest part of the journey. The highway was one of the major arteries—and assets—of the State. It stretched from the southern counties, where it was chopped off sheer by the Wall below Iselin, all the way up to Spring Valley in the north, where it was possible, after a break, to take another old road up to Newburgh and Kingston Center. It'd been cleared of rubble and occasional blockages by a massive project during the Restoration, and now it was zealously guarded by the State—there would be SI garrisons every fifteen or twenty miles along its length.

The whistle hooted once, and Brigault went up to relieve the captain. In a moment, Willis came back along the spine, massaging the tension out of his shoulder. He squatted down next to Hanson. He was still carrying the rifle; on caravan, it was chained to his wrist, and it never left him—he even slept with it. It was nearly irreplaceable, and worth more than some of the cargo. That reminded Hanson of Oristano's revolver, wrapped heavily in oilskin and hidden in Hanson's pouch—Gossard's idea; he'd never've had the presence of mind to think of it. Stealing the revolver was alone enough to earn him the death penalty; in fact it was probably a more serious offense than the killing of Oristano. Thinking that, Hanson smiled. They could only hang him once, after all.

He greeted the captain, and they talked of the trivial things people talk of when something is making them uncomfortable in each other's presence. Imperceptibly, Willis edged the conversation around, and, after a while, Hanson realized that Willis was fishing for more information on why he was leaving Orange. To get the ride, he'd told Willis a compendium of half-truths about being laid off and blacklisted, and that he was leaving, simply, to survive. Willis knew of the enmity between Oristano and Hanson, and the tale was credible enough, except for Hanson's desire to leave Orange *immediately*, with only the clothes on his back. He had explained that away as a desire to avoid possible further prosecution by Oristano—since, as a blacklistee, he was outside the law and anyone could do anything at all to him with perfect impunity from the State—and the fact that he stood a better chance of getting a ride from Willis than from another captain. It was a good story, but Hanson was a poor liar, and Willis was very sharp. Hanson had no way of knowing how much of the story Willis believed, if he believed any of it.

"So what will you do now?" Willis asked. "You have any plans at all?"

"No," Hanson said, "just to get out of Orange, is all. I a'n't got a chance in Hell there. Upcountry, at least maybe I can get some kind of piss-ass job, someway. Don't know what, but I'm a dead man if I stay."

"Ayah," Willis said, "that's true, right enough." He sighed. He was a tall, lanky man, about ten years older than Hanson, with a face like a weathered stone hatchet. His hair was heavily streaked with gray, but he held his squatting position effortlessly, rocking slightly heel-to-toe to balance against the motion of the transport. He turned his head and stared steadily at Hanson. He had an intricate, compassionate face, but it was a grim one nevertheless—there was something unshakable in it, as cold and hard as flint. It was a face of a man accustomed to command and in the habit of depending on no one or nothing other than himself. "That's true," he repeated musingly. He shrugged, and ponderously aimed his face away from Hanson, as if it was very heavy and moved on hinges. But his eyes flicked back again. His eyes were a restless, glittering black, like those of a magpie or an ancient crow. They would fix on something, absorb it completely, flick to something else. "What was it you said you got canned for?" he asked.

"Didn't say," Hanson said. Then he told him, making

it up as he went along. He wasn't very good at this sort of thing, and he had the feeling that he was floundering in deeper and deeper. Probably he had contradicted himself a half dozen times already; it was hard to remember what he'd said even a moment ago. He was numb and confused and deeply sad, and that desperate, hysterical depression was building up again—he could feel it crying and yammering inside his belly, like a little trapped animal. He finished his story and sat resignedly, waiting to see if Willis was going to challenge him on it.

"Ayah," Willis said at last, "a bad thing." His eyes flicked away from Hanson, flicked back, flicked away. "A shame and a Goddamned waste," he said. "Piss your life away—" He stopped, sighed, scratched his ear with his finger, sighed again. After a long pause he said, "Making good time tonight."

"Ai," Hanson said.

"Ayah," Willis said.

They fell silent.

Another caravan was coming down the highway toward them, probably headed south to Orange. This one was hauled by one of the clumsy steam-tractors, puffing and clattering horrendously, belching fire-shot clouds of black smoke, its great pistons thudding back and forth. It sounded like a giant's sackful of pots and plates being dragged across rocky ground. The two big vehicles hooted at each other as they passed. The sound rolled wistfully around the low hills until it was blotted up by the thick pine woods. Willis shifted position restlessly. He ran a hand up through his graying hair, brought it down to tug at his earlobe, but didn't say anything after all. Hanson was aware that Willis was wrestling with some complex emotion, but there was no way to tell exactly what it was. They sat silently while the transport clicked up a slight rise. To the west, the country opened out into extensive piney woods, but to the east, Hanson knew, there was nothing but five or six miles of low, weed-overgrown rubble, the tangled ruins of broken Utopian buildings, inhabited only by coyotes, chimeras—sports too gene-scrambled even to be regarded as human—and abandoned children who had grown up completely feral. Even the bandits preferred to camp in the woods usually. It was safer there, in spite of the wolves and the killercatchers.

Then they topped the rise and they could see the Wall itself, immense, smoldering with pinks and coral-reds, burning without flame: the Wall of the City of God. Running roughly parallel with the highway here, only five miles away, it looked almost close enough to touch. But your hand would burn, Hanson thought. It would surely burn.

"Lookit that, now," Willis said.

"Ai," Hanson said, mistaking the emotion in Willis's voice. His own heart had thudded painfully at first sight of it, and his breath had sucked in, in spite of himself. "It's very beautiful."

Willis turned to look at Hanson. His eyes had slitted up and somehow, subtly, he seemed to be crouching now, where before he had been merely squatting. He stared long and intently at Hanson. Then he made a small disgusted sound in his throat and turned back to look at the Wall. His eyes had widened, and the radiance of the Wall was reflected in them in tiny burning highlights. When he spoke again, his voice was flat and hard. "I hate it," he said. And he spat, emphatically, in the direction of the Wall. And he got up and walked back to the cab, without another word.

Hanson sat up awhile, trying to puzzle it out. But exhaustion, long denied, rolled over him like a mountain coming down, and he tied himself to a stanchion with his belt, and he went to sleep.

He awoke briefly as they were crossing the Passaic, and he realized that the sound of the whistle signaling to the SI garrison had been wailing through his dreams. He had pictured it as the cry of a huge black bird, wings wide, falling blind through the encrusted and ornamental air. Then his head lolled, and he slept.

He woke again, later, surrounded by motion and blackness. The Wall still blazed across the world, burning its image into the jelly of his retinas. He closed his eyes against the light.

And opened them again at dawn. They were in the process of crossing the Hudson, at Montgomerytown, where a bridge had survived enough intact to be capable of repair by the artisans of the Great Restoration. The Wall was no longer visible, though afterimages of it seemed to smolder in Hanson's still sleep-fogged mind. It had begun its great slow curve east of north, crossing the Hudson below Ossining—cutting straight across the water, the river disappearing under the Wall and out of the knowledge of men. Some said that the river met the sea at last, behind the Wall, inside the City of God. But no one Hanson knew had ever seen the ocean—with the possible exception of Willis—and it was a thing as impossible to picture as the City itself. Occasionally a fishing-boat or a canoe would be swept under the Wall by the current, but the crews never returned, and the river kept its secret.

Here the Hudson ran swift and fierce, as if impatient for its translation into the realms of the Divine, at Ossining. It was a wet, chilly morning. A breeze skimmed silver mists from the broad, gunmetal surface of the river; they boiled up around the black iron of the bridge, and swirled off into the lightening upper air. The sun was just climbing over a forest ridge to the east, sending broad fans of smoky light slantwise through the mist, striking bright highlights from the oily, turbulent water. The span boomed hollow under the transport, buzzed, boomed, buzzed. They were in the middle of the bridge, with everything gray and raw blue and silver-orange, the sky opening into hot gold east, night dying away to the west, the river rolling a humped shoulder below. Hanson felt something move inside, something slip, like a landslide in his head; he was leaving everything he'd ever known, everyone he'd ever known, behind. Then up the steep, thick-wooded slope of the opposite bank, and time for one last look back at the Hudson as it wound toward Ossining, back over all the lands stretching away toward Orange, where he had kept his life. Beaded with cold dew and slapped by raw morning wind, Hanson wondered if he felt regret or relief. And could not decide. And the river sank away behind, and was gone.

~

Early that evening, the transport rolled to a stop in a nondescript clearing in the woods. There was a pile of rubble in one corner that maybe used to be a house, and, among the weeds, a blistered tangle of Utopian machinery, made of an alloy so complexly specific to its task that it had no value even to the scavengers that ranged out from the cities and smallest towns of York like starveling dogs in search of something, anything, that would keep their worthless lives going yet another day. It had memory, down to the molecular level; you could melt it down and pour it into ingots, but, cooling, it would re-form itself into its original shape.

Much like a man's life, Hanson thought—you could melt it down in the fire, change it completely, but old habits and old ways of thought would re-form it again in the same pattern somewhere else. Once a loser, always a loser. Once a fool, always a fool.

Hanson took advantage of the stop to hop down off the deckplates and make his way into the musky-smelling stand of staghorn sumac by the rubble-midden and take a leak. His piss steamed in the cold evening air, and tiny clodhoppers rose to the surface of the ground to soak in it, preening, pirouetting with evident pleasure and spreading their miniature fans wide. Willis had disappeared around the back of the transport, and Brigault stayed with the cab, face set into bored immobility.

Willis's irascible voice sounded. "Hanson! Git on back here!"

"A'right. Coming!" Hanson shook free the last drop of pee, buttoned his trousers, and trudged around to the back of the transport.

Willis raised the rifle and pointed it right at his gut.

A kind of sizzle passed through Hanson, a cold and stinging surge of fear. As quietly as he could, he said, "What's this about?"

"You *know* what it's about." Willis held the rifle steady, no posturing, and no way he could miss at this distance, a man to whom the gun held no glamour but was just another tool to be used with a minimum of waste-motion and fuss.

"Listen," Hanson said, and then lapsed into silence. What could he possibly say? That numb despair and resignation were seeping back in, soaking into his bones the way his piss had soaked into the black dirt and the preening hoppers, making it impossible for him to speak. He knew that he should plead for his life, but he couldn't summon the energy to do it. He should have known that he could never get away, never get free of the morass of Orange and the mess he'd made of his life. He should have known that everything would catch up to him, that the world would reach out and crush him as casually as he would crush a bug. He *had* known that, in fact, known it with a fatalism that was deeply ingrained in the marrow of his bones. He'd fooled himself into forgetting it for a moment, into letting himself feel a moment of relief and hope, and now the retribution when it came, when Willis squeezed the trigger of the rifle and the bullet ripped his body apart, would be even more bitter and black by comparison. His luck had never been good; he'd allowed himself to think for a while that it was turning, but now, as he should have known it would, it had run out entirely instead. He cursed himself for the hundred opportunities he'd let go by to slip over the side of the transport and disappear into the wilderness between towns, where he might have carved out a living of some sort for himself. He had a gun, there were brigands he could join . . . But now it was too late. Maybe it always had been too late.

After all, what did it really matter? If Willis didn't kill him now, sooner or later the Crab in his belly *would*.

They stared at each other over the sights of Willis's rifle. A wind came up and swirled dust around Hanson's feet.

For what seemed like a very long time, neither man spoke.

At last Willis nodded to the side. Hanson's knapsack sat there, in the shadow of the transport, old and frayed, pathetically small. "You're family," Willis said, "of sorts. Blood's thicker'n water, they say. Can't bring myself to kill you. But I won't let myself be used neither."

Hanson nodded, said nothing. The moment of crisis wasn't over; he knew that there was still time for Willis to change his mind.

"A man like you," Willis said. "A man like you—" Instead of finishing the thought, he noisily cleared his throat and spat a great gob of phlegm to the side. Then, raising his voice, he shouted, "Brigault! Get off yer thumb and let's get out of here!"

As Willis strode off Hanson noticed for the first time that he had a slight limp, a stiffness in one leg that caused him to pull up slightly at the top of each stride. Willis was getting old, too. They were all getting old. To match the world, which was itself old, old and worn-out and weary, grown gray with the dust of millions of generations of lives and stained black with the residue of innumerable sins.

3

HANSON STOOD THERE for a long time, staring at the train pulling away until it had dwindled to a distant string of moving red jewels, and then, after it had vanished completely, at the empty road itself, a gray streak through blackness.

The night gathered around him. Crows exploded up out of the trees on the crest of a distant hill, startled by some noise in the forest, wheeling against the darkening sky and crying out harshly as they flew, in some guttural language he could not understand, finally settling back down into the treetops again. Then there was only silence, broken occasionally by the soughing of the wind through the trees, and by the distant and plaintive chime-like sobbing of some unknown creature far away among the trees in the dark.

At last, when he could stand the quiet and the black eventlessness no longer, he stooped to pick up his knapsack. The gun was still there, wrapped in his second pair of trousers. He stuck it in his belt.

There was a trail, hardly more than a deer run, that

ran through the clearing here at right angles to the road, and briefly he vacillated between the two directions it proffered him. Then, because it hardly mattered, he chose one at random, and started walking.

~

The sun had gone out of the sky entirely now, the last orange cloud of sunset guttering from red to purple-gray to sullen black, and only the soft light from the Wall suffused the wood, flushing it with an unearthly coral glow that cast strange iridescent shadows with blood red edges. Hanson had been traveling for hours, following the trail through the rubble of Utopian ruins, imperishable foundations filled with waters rust-red and turquoise-blue from chemical poisons leached out of the surrounding soil, and the occasional rotting and incomprehensible machine, the remnants of a centuries-long Retreat from the bright dwellings of the Utopians. He pushed his way through woods spotted with feral ornamentals and fruit trees that over the ages had drifted away from their original functions and now produced fruit indigestible to human stomachs . . . or that perhaps had been designed in the first place to feed unknown and long-vanished races, strange and inhuman races that had been so thoroughly forgotten that neither their names nor even the memory of their presence had survived, save only for the trees. In all this time, he had seen nobody and arrived nowhere, but only walked, unthinking, like an automaton.

Then he saw the glint of firelight up ahead.

He stopped. Whoever or whatever was before him, it was probably best to avoid them altogether. Only outlaws, bandits, or worse would be out in these unwholesome ruins. Honest men would have no reason to be here.

Thinking this, he could almost have laughed. He had nothing in common with honest men anymore. He was an outlaw himself now, cast out from human company like a manshogger or pariah dog.

In the darkness, somebody coughed.

Hanson stiffened in astonishment. The cough had been quiet and deliberate, a noise he was *meant* to hear. There was a lookout guarding the path, unseen, and he had just been warned that if he tried to turn away now, he was as good as dead. No help for it, he had to go forward, follow the light to its source, seek common cause with whatever human refuse clustered about its warmth. He belonged there now, after all, didn't he?

Pushing through a stand of bamboo, he entered a clearing. Dark forms hunkered about the campfire, as stolidly motionless as so many apes. They looked up incuriously at his approach, firelight flickering in their eyes. There were at least a dozen of them, perhaps as many as fifteen or sixteen; the half-light, guttering and then flaring again sporadically, made it hard to tell exactly. The pale, near-human corpse of a thant, spitted on a stick, was roasting over the fire. The peculiar stench of the roasting meat filled the clearing, thick and pungent and strange, hovering uneasily somewhere between appetizing and nauseating.

With a swagger he did not feel, Hanson strode into the light, ostentatiously loosening the gun in his belt, making sure they all got a good look. Paradoxically, the bright fire gathered darkness about itself, blinding him, making him perfectly vulnerable. He cleared his throat. "Who's boss here?"

For a long moment nobody moved. It was as if he had asked a deeper and more profound question than they were prepared to address, as if he'd challenged them to count the stars in the sky or riddle him the meaning of human pain or draw a street map of the City of God.

He was sweating now; the fire seemed to roar up inside of him. He kept one hand firm on the butt of the revolver, though it was really useless here—easiest thing in the world to come up from behind and brain him with a rock if that's what they had a mind to do. The gun, the fabulously valuable gun, only made him so much less secure, for it gave them something to gain from his death.

Under the pervasive woodsmoke and the unsettling odor of the roasting thant, he could smell where they went to shit, not bothering even to put a decent distance between themselves and their leavings, and this told him a great deal about the sort of men they were. Careless men. Irresponsible men. He felt a gut-deep disapproval of the lot of them. Even outlaws—no, make that *especially* outlaws—needed discipline.

But they were dangerous nonetheless, perhaps even more dangerous for that very lack of discipline.

A frighteningly ordinary-looking man stood up. "Name's Mahoney." He looked a little to either side, as a man with dogs might, if he were not perfectly secure in his control of his hounds. "Ye're a far way from home."

"Ayah." As nonchalantly as he could, Hanson said, "Looking for someone to hook up with."

Mahoney considered the gun, looked at the imposing size and bulk of Hanson, and drew the obvious conclusions. "Ever kill a man?"

Hanson nodded slowly. "I guess." The words hung heavy before him. It was the first time he had admitted his terrible crime aloud.

Mahoney twisted his hand strangely and a knife appeared in it. He walked toward and then past Hanson, to the remains of the thant charring over the fire, and sliced off a slab.

"Go back to your post," he said to the still-unseen man behind Hanson. Then he thrust the meat into Hanson's hands. "Eat."

~

So it was, with a one-word command and a mouthful of meat so repugnant that he barely managed to force it down, that Hanson joined the band of outlaws. He was ravenous, but after that first bite, he quietly set the meat aside. He had proved his obedience. Maybe tomorrow there'd be something more wholesome to eat. And if not . . . well, he'd see.

Suddenly, a little man leaped up on top of a log to the smoky side of the campfire. The firelight leaped and jumped on his sunken features, and he worked his loose and toothless mouth for a bit before he spoke. "Praise God!" he cried. Then, lowering his voice so that he was speaking almost confidentially, "We are all of us insane. And yet, it is not our fault!"

With good-natured disdain, the outlaws turned to look at him.

"We can't help it. It's the Wall's fault. Its existence forces us to acknowledge that our reality is out of phase with our desires. But we cannot admit this. We *cannot.* So, in denying it, we go mad. This is called cognitive dissonance."

Sitting on the log beside him, Mahoney grinned wolfishly. "The Preacher's in one of his moods. This oughta be good."

"Angels used to walk the Earth, indistinguishable among men. They could pass through the Wall at will, because they had subjugated themselves to the will of Heaven. And, if angels could do so, then why not you and I?"

"Tell it, Preach," one of the men said sardonically.

Encouraged, the little man waved his arms. He spoke feverishly, with a passionate intensity. "Man and Heaven must be reconciled. Once I was a great man, a worldly man, learned in all the things that did not matter. I spent my days among the archives of Harrisburg. Until finally I realized that Reconciliation was my destiny, and began the search for the key." He looked around to either side. "And I found it!" he said triumphantly. "I found the key to Heaven, and I hold it within me. Right in here!" He slapped his chest enthusiastically. "It's wrapped around my heart, dearer than life, closer than breath, and it will open the—" He faltered and paused. "Open the—" His voice trailed off, and he looked around vaguely. "What was I about to—?"

One of the men pursed his lips and made a lewd sucking noise. The others laughed uproariously. The light of fanaticism went out of the little man, his face collapsing into pathos and misery, body slumping like a balloon with a slow leak.

Hanson felt sickened. There was only one reason such a group of men would tolerate this broken creature. Worse, to survive here, to gain their acceptance, to be recognized as one of their kind, a man who didn't set himself above his fellows, he would have to avail himself of the Preacher's services as well. And he didn't think he could. There were limits, there had to be limits, to what a man would do to survive. Let it pass, he told himself, nobody's expecting you to do anything tonight, no sense borrowing trouble.

Not much more was said that evening. A joke or two, the purport of which was beyond Hanson's comprehension, some lifeless verbal scuffling between two men whose hatred for each other aroused no passion, and some quiet, inconsequential talk about a planned raid on an outlying farmhouse—Hanson got the impression that the ambitions of these men did not extend very far. They were as good as dead already, and most likely knew it. Thinking about things would only make them worse.

Mahoney leaned close and spoke into his ear. "Tomorrow," he said quietly, "I'll need you to take care of a little problem for me." Drawing back, he gave Hanson a sharp look to make sure he understood.

"A'right," Hanson said. Maintaining an outward calm, though his heart was pounding like a jackhammer. He understood well enough. He had just agreed to kill a man and he didn't even know *who*.

Mahoney blew his breath out noisily. "That's a'right then." He stood briskly, and slapped Hanson on the back. "We sleep in the ruins. Pick yourself out a spot."

He disappeared into the darkness. Several of the others were already gone.

So they had not even bothered to build themselves shelters. Somehow Hanson was not surprised. He scouted out a flat spot in the angle of two ancient walls, and laid out his blanket preparatory to sleep.

The Preacher came stumbling around the corner, stopped, and stood blinking and bewildered. "This is—" he began. "I was—that is, I was sleeping here and I, I—" His mouth opened and closed, gulping against tears.

Disgusted with the little monkey-faced creature, Hanson gathered up his blanket. "Oh, hell," he grumbled. "Take it, if y' want it. I'll find another spot." He left, sickened by the pathetically grateful expression that flooded the Preacher's face, the moist and worshipful look that came into his eyes.

~

Hanson was caught in an endless, looping dream when the raid began. He was on the transport again, rolling up and down to the rhythm of life on the roads. It was a long, easy rhythm; it lent itself to a watchful contemplation that was an edge away from sleep, and yet was almost preternaturally alert. There was nothing to mark it but the passage of the sun, rolling up across the arch of sky, under the horizon, up again, and the roads themselves, slipping endlessly under the transport, sometimes paved, sometimes mud, sometimes sunbaked and dusty, the trees along the roadside white with the dust kicked up by the transport, as if they had been hit by a blizzard in the midst of summer. The heat would be rising in waves from the deckplates, shimmering vision. The sky would be dazzlingly blue, and the sun a hot copper penny in it, except when the dust-trail would shift and swirl around the transport itself, and then the sky would become dirty white, and the masked sun would become a smoldering bloodshot eye. Always the endless moving ribbon of the road sliding smoothly toward them, being swallowed by the prow of the transport, with new road always coming into being ahead of them, around the next curve or over the next hill, sliding forward to be swallowed in its turn. And occasionally a hamlet or village, borne up by the current of the road, bobbing nearby for an instant, and then whirled away behind, like a drowsy, peasant-infested, cow-carrying chip of driftwood. He would become aware that he had dreamed this before and then immediately lose all assurance that this was so. So he would anxiously relive the nonevents of traveling the roads, the muted waterfall thunder of the engine, the constant swaying of the transport and the relentless thudding of the treads, the trees, the road, the villages, Willis's grunted orders, Brigault's sudden and pointless laughter. Until he forgot what he was worrying about and it all began again.

He awoke to explosions.

Men were shouting, screaming, running. A bullet splintered bark from a tree not five yards from him and there were bright lights and dark shapes beyond the dying embers of the campfire, down the path up which he had come. Savage shouts echoed through the ruins, and another bullet sizzled through the air.

In a panicked instant, Hanson was on his feet, quivering and frozen motionless, like a jack-lighted deer. Somebody slammed into him, cursed, and was gone, along with Hanson's paralysis. He grabbed at his shirt to keep from losing the gun, which he'd carefully stuck between undershirt and belt before turning in. It did not occur to him to use it.

Stumblingly at first, and then faster, he began to run.

Men were shouting and crashing into things, running ahead of him, up the path. He followed blindly. Somebody grabbed his arm and he lashed out without looking, his fist smashing into a face. But whoever it was did not let go, but wrapped both arms around his waist.

Turning, he stared down into the Preacher's fearful face.

"Don't!" the Preacher gasped. "For God's sake, don't! That's just what they *want* you to do. They're just beaters. The SIs will be up the trail, waiting. I've seen it before! And politicians—it's a sport to them, ambushing rievers, they get to notch bandits without any risk to themselves. Sometimes they take souvenirs."

The old man's unexpected lucidity broke through the haze of fear and instinct. Hanson stopped and looked around. A flare screamed high into the night. Bright lights, harsh shadows. "What should we do?"

"We've got to get away from the path," the Preacher said. "This way." Tugging at Hanson's arm, he half pulled him over a pile of crumbling bricks and between two ruined walls. Awkwardly, Hanson let himself be led. Behind them, two SIs stooped over a fallen bandit, machetes in hand, hacking wildly, the blades flashing in the smoky light from the Wall as they rose and fell, rose and fell. One SI looked up and, seeing them, shouted.

~

They struggled deeper into the darkness.

Together he and the Preacher forced their way through a nightmare of noise-filled woods, stumbling over low walls, ducking under loops of vampire weed and blundering into tangles of mile-a-minute vines, flinching every time a bullet pierced the air with its shrill whine or a phased sonics cannon blanketed the area with an awful split-second of unbearable silence. There was nothing but fear and confusion in Hanson's mind. He'd left his knapsack behind. He had nothing now but his gun and the clothes on his back.

Then the Preacher fell and did not get up.

"Stand, damn you!" Hanson seized the Preacher's shoulder to give him an impatient shake, but his hand came away wet and sticky. He looked at it wonderingly.

Blood.

He stared down at the wrinkled old man, saw the grayness in his bruised face, how the clothes down one side of his body were black with blood. He'd been wounded all along, kept going by hysteria and fear. A flare went up in the air, and doubled shadows from it and the Wall danced in all directions. The little man wasn't going to make it. It was a miracle he'd lasted this long. Hanson couldn't take him along, wherever he was going—it would be useless.

The Preacher needed a doctor, and Hanson had no doctoring in him; he could splint a leg or tie a tourniquet, and had several times, back at the factory, but that was it—the kind of gunshot wound the Preacher had was far beyond him. Best to keep moving and let the Preacher fend for himself as best he could, live or die as the gods willed. There was no time now for *sentiment* . . .

Cursing himself for a fool even as he did it, Hanson bent down and scooped the little man up in his arms.

"They killed an angel in Harrisburg," the Preacher said suddenly. He did not open his eyes. "It's in the records—not that anybody but me ever bothered to read the records . . . Used to do that a lot, back then, the angels. Angels passing through the Wall . . ."

"Don't talk," Hanson said. He started walking, too tired, too burdened, to run any more. If the SIs caught him, they caught him. It was hard even to care.

But the Preacher went on unheeding. "So close . . . I came so very *close*. I was not an inconsequential man . . . but I was afraid. Couldn't take those final steps. I had the key to Heaven in me, and I couldn't *go*." He started to weep. "At night, I hear its voice, calling, calling . . . it's never *still*. I'm going to die, aren't I?"

Embarrassed, Hanson repeated, "Don't talk."

"Take me to the Wall," the Preacher said, with surprising force. "I want to get that far at least. Bury me there. So

I can say I went the distance."

"Yah, sure." Hanson's step was slowing, and the weight of the body in his arms seemed heavy beyond endurance. He didn't think he could go much farther. The night, so full of noise for the duration of their flight, now sank back down into silence, either because of distance or because the SIs and their political masters had finished having their fun and departed.

They came upon an overgrown Utopian road over which meandered a narrow trail, probably not even human-made but rather something created by coyotes or wyverns or thants as they wandered in their dream-sunk and instinctual rounds, and Hanson decided that it could not possibly be the same as the one that passed through the bandit camp. At any rate, safe or not, he was tired of fighting his way through the brush. The woods were preternaturally silent, not so much as a cricket or a knacker stirring. The only sound came from the Wall, a soft humming and buzzing like an infinite swarm of bees heard from a million miles away.

Abruptly, the Preacher gave a shudder and went still in his arms. With a cold seizure of the heart, Hanson knew that he was dead. He stared down at the man, so small, so light, and as he stared, a metal rod burst out of the Preacher's chest, passing through skin and muscle and cloth as if they did not exist, gleaming, quicksilver fast.

It bent, unfolded several joints, and then plunged into Hanson.

With a cry of horror, he stumbled back, slapping wildly at his chest with both hands, letting the Preacher's corpse fall to the ground. The rod had already disappeared into him as completely as if it had never been there, sinking out of sight within his chest, leaving no trace of its existence behind.

It was gone.

Hanson was tempted to dismiss the incident, the bizarre *thing* that had leaped out at him like some monstrous jack-in-the-box and then plunged *into* his body as easily as a hot knife going through butter, dismiss it as a hallucination brought on by fear and fatigue. But he could *feel* it inside him, a heavy weight in his chest that shifted his center of balance and altered his movements in subtle ways. He felt a different man with it in him, estranged from his own body, an exile sitting within the control-cab of his skull, staring horrified and dispassionate out of the eye-sockets. Worse, he could feel the device's desires like a burden of guilt or regret gnawing at the back of his mind. It was anxious to go home, and told him so not in words but in a cold mechanical yearning so intense he felt naked and near-helpless before it.

He stood shivering for a long moment, then bent and picked the Preacher back up again.

The Wall was not far distant, a hundred yards or half a mile, he could not tell. But not far. All the woods around him blazed with its preternatural glow. He walked toward it, impelled by the horror behind him, by the burden in his arms, and by the alien machinery now wrapped around his heart. He could not help himself.

Up close, only a few steps away, closer than he'd ever heard of anyone coming to it, the Wall refused to resolve itself into solid substance. Little flickering motes of intense reddish-pink light swirled and crawled over each other, and the humming sound, though no louder than before, passed right through him; his entire body buzzed and vibrated like the sounding board of a guitar. The Wall loomed so high now that when he craned his head, it seemed to fill the universe, and he had the vertiginous sensation of falling into it. The thing in his chest seemed to leap up with joy.

I won't, he thought wildly. *I refuse!* But he kept walking. The Wall filled his sight entirely, that terrible, unearthly dazzle. Briefly, he tried to lie to himself, to pretend that he was just going to bring the Preacher to the Wall he had spent his entire life journeying toward without ever reaching, and place his body there before it, like an offering to an angry God, so that He might be moved to pity and forgive His sinning children, especially that one in particular who was named Hanson.

But being so close to the Wall seemed to lend the key strength; the buzzing rose up and overwhelmed Hanson's thoughts in a great wave.

A hole opened in the Wall like a mouth, directly before him. It was big enough for a man to walk into. *No,* he thought. *No*!

He walked in.

The Wall closed behind him. He was in a moving bubble that kept pace with him. The walls provided enough light for him to see by and enough air to breathe. But it was warm, much warmer than the air outside had been. Sweat beaded up on his forehead, ran in rivulets from his armpits. It was ungodly *hot* in here! He kept walking, but more slowly now. His arms ached dreadfully, and his knees were starting to buckle. He cursed his weakness, hefted the Preacher's body, and forced himself forward.

He kept walking straight ahead, until he was sure he should have passed through by now. How thick *was* the Wall anyway? How thick could it possibly *be*? The swarming buzz of microscopic bees made it hard for him to think.

On an impulse, he turned and walked at right angles to his previous path. The bubble tracked him perfectly. So it wasn't guiding him! He returned, as best he could, to his previous path. But he was definitely lost now, somewhere within the reaches of the Wall, and it was growing hotter. His skull buzzed and stuttered, and his breath came in long, shuddering gasps. It was as hot as the inside of an oven. He was surprised that his hair hadn't caught fire.

The Preacher's body grew heavier and heavier. His step faltered, grew slower and slower, as though he were wading through mud. Finally, he stopped, and, groaning, sank to his knees in despair. The buzzing grew louder. He reached out a hand, and where his palm brushed against the glowing substance of the Wall, it suddenly stung like a thousand wasps. He whipped his hand back, and saw that it was all bloody, skin and flesh sliced away where he had brushed it against the Wall. Ignoring the pain, he extended the arm again, gingerly, index finger extended.

As he'd suspected, the second time he didn't have to reach so far. The bubble was closing about him. There must be something he could do to stop its progress, but with the heat and noise increasing unbearably, he could not think what it was. He could not think. He could only sink down over the Preacher's corpse, grateful that his ordeal was almost over, as the bubble dwindled around him and its molten substance wrapped itself about his skin in sudden and searing pain.

Hanson screamed.

4

HE AWOKE IN DAYLIGHT, lying on his back in a meadow, shaded by an elm tree bearing vivid orange fruit. A gentle breeze touched him. It carried the mingled scents of sandalwood and wintergreen.

A tall, inhumanly thin man in a charcoal gray tunic stood watching over Hanson. He had a kind face. On seeing Hanson awake, he smiled. "Welcome home," he said.

Home? Hanson rolled over and levered himself up on an elbow, and then rose to his feet. He looked around and knew for a certainty that he had passed all the way through the Wall.

Heaven was not as he'd imagined it.

No, that was wrong. Hanson had never been able to imagine *what* Heaven might actually be like. Oh, when he was young, he'd been as free with a crudely ribald speculation as anyone, but as far as what it might be *like* to actually stand in the City of God—

Whatever it was, it wasn't this.

He looked across a vast lawn freckled with occasional pairs of silver dots or circles—gently rolling land that stretched as far as the eye could see, and all well-manicured, trimmed, as if someone were mad enough to mow it all. Not that any man could. It would've taken a hundred mowers, in constant motion, tireless, insanely devoted to their task... He shook his head. There were—*buildings?*—here and there, isolated from each other, immaculate and pointless. A cone larger than any single structure Hanson had ever seen, delicately balanced on its point and canted to one side. A red glass sphere caught in arches of congealed lightning. What could only be a baby's arm magnified a million times, sticking out of the earth, fingers gently moving in a way that was undeniably alive.

It did not look right. Hanson knew there was some *other* way that Heaven should look, though he lacked the ability to put it into words. More beautiful, somehow. More symmetrical, perhaps. It should be bizarre and wonderful and, yes, strange, certainly strange. But not like *this*. Never like this. He turned back to the thin man, who was still waiting patiently on him. "Are you . . . an angel?"

An urbane, undeniably sympathetic, and self-dismissive gesture. "I am a function. You have been in the lands of the Renunciates for so long a time that you can no longer recall your origins. Until you recover your memory, you may call upon my services as your interface and guide."

"My memory," Hanson said flatly. He could make sense of none of this.

"Your friend is anxious to see you."

He cast his mind back, awkwardly groping for meaning. Anyone who could have been counted a friend of his, by however loose a reckoning, was either long dead or left behind in Orange; he had no friends anymore, not unless you counted the Preacher, and he—"My friend is dead."

"Not any longer."

~

The Preacher sat in the grass of a nearby hollow, running a finger around and around the inside of his mouth, admiring his perfect new teeth. He smiled broadly at Hanson. "Quite a set of choppers, eh?" Then, indicating the thin man, "Don't pay any mind to Cicero. He's not real."

"He said he was a function."

"It means the same thing. I told him to let you sleep, figured you could use it. Me, I've been up for hours. How do you feel?"

"Fine," Hanson said uncomfortably. He slapped his hands together, and then, as he realized what he'd done, raised them up to his face in wonderment: the places on the palm and the tip of the one finger that the Wall had eaten away had been completely, magically healed. And, now that he thought about it, he really *did*, he felt just fine! A hundred small aches and aggravations were gone, from the sour tooth that had nagged dimly from the back corner of his mouth for as long as he could remember to the thorn scratches and sticker-rashes he'd incurred blundering into the mile-a-minute vines last night—gone, as if they had never been. He rotated his neck and it didn't make the little crackling noises that he had grown accustomed to. Even the gut-pain of the Crab, by God, even *that* was gone! Something moved deep within him, a small and hurtful aching sensation so alien to his nature that it took him a second to identify it.

Hope.

"By God," he breathed. "By God, Preacher, I—"

"Boone!" the little man snapped. "My name is J. Pickett Boone, and don't you forget it!"

Startled, Hanson looked hard at him. There was a clear light in Boone's eyes; the mental confusion of earlier was gone. He held himself like a supervisor now. Not only his body had been healed by his passage into Heaven, it seemed, but his mind as well. And with his newfound clarity of thought must surely have come memories of his association with the outlaw band, and humiliation about the services he had provided them in his long evasion of the Wall. Boone was glaring up at him with a fierce intensity, fists clenched, trembling, like a terrier-dog working itself up to attack a bull. Hanson found that he despised Boone less than before, and, paradoxically, disliked him more.

He dropped his eyes. "Didn't mean anything by it," he mumbled.

For a long, still moment, Boone's face remained closed, tight, hostile. Then he made a curt, dismissive gesture. The balance of power between them had shifted, subtly but surely; immediately, Hanson regretted having let the moment slide by the way he had. But it was too late, no use trying to put the egg back into the shell, what was done was done. The little man stood and stretched and looked searchingly about him, staring into the middle distance where the grassland rose in great arched ribs, under which birds flew and atop which were trees and grazing deer, and beyond, at the ranges of what were either strange mountains or even stranger buildings. Boone looked upon the bizarre structures of Heaven with shrewd, knowledgeable eyes; they clearly did not seem strange to *him* . . .

Cicero stood nearby with that blank, alert look of his. Hanson felt oddly reluctant to address his questions to him. Lowering his voice, he said, "Boone, I can't make any sense out of"—he swept a hand to take in everything, the buildings he could almost comprehend one at a time but could not assemble into a single coherent picture, could not seem to hold in his mind all at the same time—"all this."

"Are you a religious man?" Boone asked.

The question took him aback, it had been so long a time since anybody had asked him anything remotely like it. Religion was not the sort of thing a man like him was expected to have an opinion on. "I don't think so."

"Then maybe there's some slight chance of your understanding." The little man spoke in a fussy, professorial manner, falling back to the rhythms and cadences of his long-forgotten former life. "Hanson, the City of God isn't any such thing. Got that? It's not inhabited by gods or angels or anything of the sort, but by people. People like you and me."

"Uh . . ."

"Did you ever try to imagine what it was like to live in the time of the Utopians?"

"Well—yeah. Sure. A little, sometimes."

"Not exactly easy, was it? Once you got past having all the food and clean water you ever wanted, good clothes, a soft bed, and never having to do sweat-work again in your life, could you picture exactly what you'd be *doing* with all that wealth, all those machines, how it would feel to be a Utopian?"

Hanson shook his head.

"Well, all that—the clean water, the limitless food, the ease and comfort, heat in the winter and cool breezes in the summer that squirt out of a machine at the twist of a knob—was just the *beginning.* Wealth creates wealth and knowledge builds upon knowledge. During the era of the Utopians, knowledge went into a period of exponential increase, and, in one grand surge—from my researches, I have reason to believe it happened within the span of a single human lifetime—people gained control of such immense powers and such total freedoms that . . . Well, it *changed* them. The people who resulted from this change—let's call them the post-Utopians—would have been as incomprehensible to the Utopians as the Utopians are to us. They have wealth and power beyond your craziest dreams. Far beyond anything you even *can* imagine. They are like gods in their power, and yet they're not gods. They are only post-Utopians. Remember that. They're just people with all the technology, all the wealth, all the power anyone could ever want."

Hanson could follow what Boone was saying. He could even understand it. But somehow he could not fit his head around it, could not encompass it, could not feel and accept the truth of it. It was all too strange. He struggled to put into words some reason why he could not entirely accept it. "But—" he began.

He stopped, swallowed, tried again.

"But then—why the Wall?"

"I don't know." Boone began walking and Hanson had no choice but to follow. Cicero trailed after them like an obliging shadow. "Let's ask them."

Not many paces distant were two silver metal plates, each roughly ten feet in diameter. With no particular emphasis, Boone strolled onto one. Hanson and Cicero followed.

Something like a twisty silver pillar, a metal cyclone, shot up from the other plate into the air, disappeared into the clouds, and then with a mad looping motion came rushing down upon them. Cicero's hand squeezed Hanson's shoulder reassuringly. "Wait." He heard the word but could not parse its meaning, could not even attempt to run, could do nothing in fact but stand rooted where he was in horror. The crazy thought flitted through his head that now he knew how a mouse felt just before being stepped on by an horse, and then the cyclone slammed down upon them.

He blinked, and the pillar was gone.

Everything around him had changed. He was standing before a grove of orange-roofed mansions—palaces, almost—all raised high above the ground on impossibly thin stilts. For a giddy instant he thought they were floating, and then, when he realized the truth, feared the stilts would snap and send these massive structures smashing down upon him.

A great sphere of water hung over the stilted buildings, dwarfing them. What light came through it was wan and diminished, bathing the buildings in a wavering shadowy cool, as if they were under the sea.

"There." Cicero pointed to a balcony, high above them. "A typical dwelling, selected, as you requested, to be as like those you are familiar with as possible. This one is in the Italianate style." After a brief hesitation, Boone nodded. The silver-gray cyclone leaped up and slammed down upon them again, and they were standing on the balcony.

Hanson craned his head and stared up into the water. From here, the sphere was obviously not solid, but a bubble with walls mere yards deep, wrapped around a core of nothing. A shark swam by overhead, twisting its head from side to side, mouth opening and closing in little gasps.

A salt breeze wafted down from the bubble. Multicolored ribbons twisted and curled in the air between buildings and were gone. Staring out at a hundred other balconies, all empty, Hanson felt a sourceless, aching loneliness growing within him, the sort of emptiness one might feel in an abandoned city, an animal certainty that he was surrounded by nothing but vacancy and isolation.

"Where is everybody?" he asked.

Cicero looked regretful. "Gone."

"Gone where?"

"Elsewhere."

"I don't understand."

"They have followed... certain trends to their inevitable conclusion," Cicero said. "Would you like to go inside now?"

Boone hesitated, irresolute. "Well, as long as we're here, we might as well take a look."

Cicero walked forward, and the wall parted for him. Boone ducked after.

Hanson had no choice but to follow.

He found himself in a clean, light-filled space. The ceiling was high, the pillars thin, and the leaded-glass windows opalescent. It was a fairy-tale structure, sculpted of moonlight and mist, of soft evening shadows and ice. Even standing within it he couldn't quite bring himself to believe in its existence. It was too fine, too delicate. Hanson could not think back to a time when he'd been young enough to believe in such a place. Yet—here it was. It made him feel gross and crude by contrast, hairy and smelly as a troll, unworthy.

While he was gawking, Boone had been asking questions. Cicero was explaining to him how the cyclones worked. "—rotating you thirty-seven degrees in time, which is why it feels instantaneous; in actuality your rest-motion is only a few thousand kilometers per hour."

Boone nodded, frowning with concentration and understanding. "Similarly, this doorway is distributed in probability along a curve of thirty-nine thousand miles, so that . . ."

He led them into a room with enormous windows.

Entering, Hanson seemed to grow lighter, his movements unnaturally slow, like those of a man underwater, his head giddy with uncertainty, so that it seemed almost as if he had to push his foot down to bring it to the floor at the end of each step. Otherwise, it would've simply floated up and up, leaving him treading air.

"Where are—" Hanson began, and, somehow placing his feet badly, went tumbling over backward, his balance all *wrong* damnit, falling with impossible slowness and thrashing awkwardly as the floor came floating up toward him.

Cicero reached over to catch and steady him. "I could increase the local gravity gradient, if you wish," he said, but whatever his offer might entail, it meant nothing at all to Hanson. Boone hid an amused smile.

Flushing, Hanson looked away, through the windows.

Glorious and terrifying views! A bright gray-and-white wasteland of rocks and sand, and, in the distance, a range of humped and rounded mountains. Long black shadows stretching toward forever under the blackest of skies.

The bleached skeleton of a giraffe lay on the barren soil just outside the window.

Low over the mountains hung... something. Something round and blue and streaked with white, as distant as the Moon, but far larger than the Moon ever was.

It was the Earth. Hanson recognized it from the faded Utopian pictures that were preserved in the Courthouse back in Orange, and which a disbelieving bailiff apathetically pointed out to disbelieving visitors as proof that human beings had once, long ago, left the surface of the Earth. This looked just like those pictures, only far more vivid. The colors were unimaginably brighter, the oceans the wildest blue, the clouds dazzling!

It was unbearable.

Hanson twisted wildly away, went tumbling, and more by luck than not, grabbed the doorway with one rough hand. All in a single surge of panic, he pulled himself through and back into the first room. For a long moment, he knelt there, eyes clenched tight. Madness! How could Boone stand it? After a minute or two he gathered himself together and spoke to the backs of the other two:

"I'm going outside. Just for a minute."

They were lost in talk. Neither of them responded.

He went outside, and it was afternoon. Only a minute before, when he had entered the room, it had been morning. But there was no mistaking it—the sun, wan and silvery through the water-bubble, had risen higher, the stilted shadows of the buildings had grown longer. He had lost hours, somehow.

Weakly, Hanson leaned against the balustrade, staring not up at the marine animals or out at the bizarrely contoured horizon, but into empty space, at nothing. A tangle of colored ribbons floated in the air, twisting between buildings, a whimsical carnival brightness, and when part of it drifted by him, he reached up impulsively to touch it. One ribbon playfully wrapped itself about his wrist like a tendril, and he found himself standing on a balcony on the building opposite staring into his own startled eyes. He was in both places simultaneously, and then in a third on an entirely different building, staring out into the fields of Heaven where something like a shark's fin—triangular, dark, immense—lifted up from the grass and slowly subsided. All three Hansons were aware of the others' thoughts, but their thoughts were not identical but divergent, different in the qualities of their fear and dismay.

The ribbon released his wrist, and he was one and alone again.

He lurched back from the balustrade and across one of the silver plates. A cyclone slammed down on him.

Then off.

~

When Hanson stumbled from the plate, he found himself in a windblown hall. Down its center, unsupported, hung a line of vast stone bells. They were as gray and rough-looking as granite, but when he wonderingly reached up a finger to touch one, it *boomed* as if struck by a maul, a deep and despairing vibration that shook his body like the sound of God sobbing.

"Naw." He stepped back from the bell, shaking his head, profoundly disturbed by something he could not put a name to. "Not like that. Naw, not like—that."

At the far end of the hall was another pair of circles—more cyclone plates. He hurried toward them, shamblingly at first, then faster. The all but imperceptible breeze of his passage brushing against the bells set up an echoing clamor, a turbulent ocean of sound that surged and swelled about him, filling him with primal dread, driving him to greater speed, so that when he reached the plate he was practically running. His feet touched one circle. A metal pillar rose from the other and slammed down upon him.

~

Silence.

He was in a room full of shadows and jumbled shapes. Something shifted slightly to one side. There were other furtive movements to the other side, up ahead, just behind. With a start, Hanson realized that he was not alone. The room was filled with prowling animals, great cats the size of cougars. There was painfully little light, but they had, he thought, human faces, and they spoke with the voices of women.

"Oh, baby," one murmured, "let me rip you open."

"My fangs are long," said another.

"My claws are sharp."

"My breasts are heavy with milk."

They prowled one over the other, haunches high in the darkness, too many, the light too dim, for Hanson to determine their number. Their eyes and teeth flashed in the gloom. They were in constant motion, slinking, stalking.

"See my long pink tongue."

"Smell my hindquarters."

"Imagine my teeth piercing your lips, tearing the flesh off of your face."

"I'll make sure you suffer a long, long time."

"Oh, honey."

Their voices overlapped in a kind of moaning chorus. Their eyes materialized and disappeared behind flirtatious lashes.

"Poor baby. It's been so long since you experienced

anything with intensity."

"*We'll* make you feel something."

"I'll pull out your intestines an inch at a time—slowly, slowly."

It was terrifying. It was too much. Hanson found himself pulling in upon himself, wrapping arms about his body, shivering. It wasn't fair! He didn't know any of the rules here, any of the assumptions. *Cicero,* he thought. If only Cicero were here, he'd know what to do.

"It's all right," Cicero said. "I'm here." He strode through the cat-women as if either he or they were not entirely real, completely ignored by them all. "If you'll look down, you'll see a set of parallel lines glowing faintly on the floor. They mark a safe passage from the one plate to the other. So long as you stay between them, you're perfectly safe."

He took Hanson's arm, led him across the room.

Wobbly, Hanson allowed himself to be led. "How did you find me?" he asked. "How did you know I—?" He stopped, unable to finish the sentence.

"I am a function."

"Oh." The cat-women paced him, musky-smelling and avid-faced. Growling their lust. Ignoring them as best he could, Hanson asked, "Why? Why would anybody want—" He swept out an arm to encompass them all. "—*this*?"

"You have been a long time away indeed," Cicero said, "to have forgotten the need for such entertainments."

They stepped on the plate—

—a grove of slim buildings so tall that the rivers of water falling from their fluted tops dissolved into rainbows and mist long before they could reach the ground.

—a stone cathedral floating within a sad brown sunset, which stared at him with a hundred human eyes.

—a twilight plane where armies of metal giants fought with axes and clubs, while small and tireless servitor machines retrieved the scrap and climbed their sides to rebuild the damaged parts.

—a small room smelling of chickens and new-mown hay, where blue flames flickered over revolving bowls of mercury.

—a tangle of snakes that raised agonized heads as large as houses against a steel-plate sky.

—an incandescent mushroom cloud, strangely still and unchanging, like a snapshot of some catastrophic explosion, a frozen instant of horrified time.

The light and heat from this last were excruciating. Hanson threw a hand over his watering eyes, his stinging face, and cried, "Where are we going?"

"Why, wherever you want," Cicero said. "We have been traveling at random, while I awaited your directions."

"Then take me home."

Cicero smiled encouragingly. "And where is that?"

It was as if one of the cat-women had arisen out of nowhere to present him with a riddle encompassing the purpose and end of human life. Hanson's mind was blank; for a long moment he could think of no possible destination to offer in response. Then, "Boone," he said finally. "Take me back to Boone."

~

There was a light dusting of yellow pollen on the balcony, and a springlike coolness to the air. Cicero gestured Hanson through a doorway and into an unfamiliar room. The walls were lined with dark wood paneling and shelves of leather-bound books. Squares and scrolls hung unsupported in the air, a dozen or more, some bright with moving images, others filled with cryptic text. Boone looked up from a writing desk, and, with a wild cry, stood. Papers scattered from him like birds. He ran through the squares and scrolls as if they did not exist, and hugged Hanson with all his strength.

"Aw, now," Hanson muttered in confusion. "C'mon, now." Embarrassed, he patted the man's back once, twice, feather-light and reluctant touches.

Boone stepped back, smiling through his tears.

"Where the hell have you *been*? I stayed here, made this my camp, hoping against hope that you'd—well, that hardly matters. You're back now, that's all that matters. Only—where have you *been?*"

"I was—" Hanson spread his hands and looked down into them helplessly as if they might contain an answer that was nowhere else to be found. He did not know where he had been. "I think I found some post-Utopians." Boone started and shot him an odd look. "They were . . . strange. Like cats."

"Those were not citizens," Cicero corrected gently. "They were a function. Like me."

"Oh, shut up." Boone wiped away his tears and put his hands on his hips. He glared up at Hanson, who, abruptly and with an odd sense of dislocation, realized that he had somehow acquired a mustache and a trim little goatee. "I suppose you think that was funny? I suppose you think you can just follow whatever damn-fool notion enters your head? Well, I have news for *you*. From this moment on, you're not going anywhere without my express permission. You got that? I don't want you going to the shithouse to jerk off without telling me first."

Hanson flushed. His muscles bunched and knotted under the lash of Boone's words. He felt that all-too-familiar burning sensation at the back of his throat, the bitter fire of resentment forcibly suppressed. He could crush the little man in his bare hands, if he wanted to, and you'd think that Boone would by God respect that, would at least grant him the elementary caution one gave a manshogger or factory machine with a known history of mangling its operators. It griped him that he did not.

But he needed Boone, and they both knew it. The City of God was comprehensible to Boone in ways it was *not* to Hanson; he needed the little man's direction and guidance. Ducking his head, he felt the old habits of submission, of obedience, of silence, the reflexive knuckling under to the loudest voice, come over him like an old, heavy, and detested coat. "It was only a little while."

"A little while! Eight *months* you were gone, and you call it—" Boone's voice rose sarcastically "—a little while?"

Hanson lifted his hands, palms up, baffled. "Eight months? But—" Boone silenced him with a look. And though he was trying to hide it, there was less anger than fear in that look: fear and loneliness. Eight months Boone had spent by himself, without human company, enduring an isolation that would be a burden for even the strongest man, and would break or even kill the weak; the gods alone knew what he'd been through, or how he had withstood it.

For long minutes, Boone simply stared at him, as if

afraid he was about to turn away and stalk off once more. Then, stooping, he began to gather up his papers. "These are my notes," he said. "Oh, nothing formal, you understand. Just jottings, really. I spent the winter researching the City's records. If you want to call them that. There's enough information available here to drown in, but none of it's organized at all usefully, nothing is presented in any kind of—well, never mind." He passed a hand over his eyes, wiping them clean of tears.

"You've moved," Hanson said.

"Eh? What? Nothing of the sort!"

"The room I saw before had pillars. And windows . . ."

Boone made a dismissive gesture. "Bah! It takes nothing to reconfigure a room. You have no idea the kind of wealth that's fallen into our hands. And power—power *unimaginable* in our old lives!" Papers gathered, he stood behind his desk, tamping them into a neat stack, and, with that simple gesture, regained all of his lost authority. "But this must be bewildering to you. How to explain? Where to begin?"

He thought for a moment.

"I was wrong," Boone said. "Remember when I told you the post-Utopians were people like you and I? I was wrong. I've opened windows into their lives and . . . they were *different*. Different in ways that made them not even remotely human. I think they destroyed themselves, but I'm not sure."

"Destroyed themselves? You mean, like—suicide?"

"Possible—barely. Burned themselves out, more likely. *Transfigured* themselves, perhaps. Indications go both ways. Let me replay for you a conversation you have doubtless long forgotten." With a wave of his hand, Boone swept the squares and scrolls to either side, leaving one, bright as a window, hanging in the center of the room. Through it, Hanson saw the balcony outside and, upon it, Cicero talking to a hulking brute of a man.

"Where is everybody?" the big man asked.

(Startled, Hanson realized it was himself.)

"Gone."

"Gone where?"

"Elsewhere."

"I don't understand."

"They have followed... certain trends to their inevitable consequences."

Boone gestured brusquely, waving the scroll out of existence. "Such things I have discovered. You cannot imagine. Fantastic, incredible things! I've tasted in surrogate the ineffable pleasures the post-Utopians discovered for themselves, glimpsed darkly, as if through a scrim, their activities and preoccupations. Oh, I am not a scholar for nothing! But where have the post-Utopians *gone*? What became of them? In this one crucial respect, I am as ignorant as you." He turned to Cicero: "Let me ask you again: Where have they gone?"

"Elsewhere."

"Where elsewhere?"

"You would not understand."

"Are they dead?"

"No."

"Will they ever come back?"

"They never went away."

"The hell with you!" To this point the exchange had proceeded with the lifeless quality of a catechism, a rote repetition of questions and answers unvarying and long committed to memory. But now Boone stood, and, hands behind his back, savagely strode to and fro, as if building up his courage. There was a wild light in his eyes. Finally he asked, "Will we see them again in recognizable form—as something roughly human, capable of communicating and interacting with us?"

"By the nature of what happened," Cicero said, "that cannot be."

"You see?" Boone turned triumphantly to Hanson. "You *see?* The City of God—its buildings and parks, its powers and potentials, the land, the sea, everything—is *ours*. Ours to control, ours to command. It belongs to *us*!"

Hanson glanced uneasily at Cicero.

Cicero said nothing, waited patiently.

"I dunno," Hanson said. It didn't seem *right* to him, somehow, to make such claims. It didn't seem safe. In his experience, everything had a price, even things you didn't get, and that price was always more than any sane man would agree to pay, given the choice. Not that you ever *got* the choice. The balance was enforced from afar, by powers immaterial and unlocatable, nothing you could even identify, much less get your hands on. "Maybe we oughta just take our time here, not do anything rash."

"No! I've waited too long. Your coming back now is a *sign*. We have to act immediately, right now, without delay." With a slash of one hand, Boone made all the scrolls and squares disappear. The room looked monkishly bare without them. Turning to Cicero, he said, "Take us to the Throne of God."

"The local utility node, you mean?"

"Whatever you want to call it—bring us there."

Cicero nodded. "As you wish."

5

THE THRONE WAS LOCATED in a windowless zone like a jet bead atop a slanted glass tower whose stairs took them a terrifying half hour to climb. From a distance, the tower looked like a syringe with a black drop of blood at its tip. Within, the walls and stairs alike were transparent, marked only by gleams of reflected and refracted light, making the ascent a sickeningly vertiginous experience. There was no other way to reach it, Cicero explained, because the powers it controlled were too great to be tapped on a whim, even a post-Utopian's whim. At the top, within a hideously unstable region of blackness, they confronted the thing itself—an unornamented silver chair with armrests and a high back.

Boone had been here before.

"Control," Boone said. "Even the City of God needs to be controlled. *Especially* the City of God." He paced back and forth before the Throne, talking rapidly and with an unnatural energy. "There are many such towers, each tapping a fraction of the power of the Wall and responsible for the maintenance of a small segment of the lands within. From this chair, one man can control more power than is held by all the mortal nations combined. I have often come here to meditate upon whether to assume responsibility for that power."

"*Don't!*" Hanson said suddenly. He couldn't explain the wave of apprehension that came over him, the fearful certainty that Boone was about to destroy them both; but he felt it nevertheless, down to the soles of his feet. "Just—don't *do* it!"

Boone nodded, not listening. He stopped pacing and struck a pose, hands behind back, legs wide. "Hanson, we stand on the brink of history. It is our duty to humanity—our destiny, even—to tear down the Wall separating the Human Domain from the City of God." He stared at the Throne without seeming to actually see it, his eyes gleaming and blank with excitement.

"Think of it, Hanson! For ages, we have been made helpless, impoverished by the presence of a City whose accomplishments we could never hope to duplicate, whose very existence made a mockery of all our aspirations. Now . . . now, we can make the Earth a garden, abolish human misery, free men to follow their better natures. We'll fill the skies and roads with great vessels again, millions of them! We'll build cities—*human* cities!—on the Moon, beneath the seas, at the poles. Can you *picture* it, Hanson?"

Hanson dumbly shook his head.

Boone laughed, a shallow, brittle laugh. "No. No, of course you can't. But you'll see—you'll *see*." He took a step toward the Throne, then convulsively whirled about, and, hugging himself, said, "It is a great responsibility I am assuming here, a terrible burden indeed. You see that, don't you? By its very nature power must be apportioned, divided, distributed—and withheld. That is natural law. Fanatics and opportunists, the self-serving and corrupt, will be drawn to this point like moths to the flame. We must take steps to ensure that this power does not fall into the wrong hands."

In all the crawling and uneasy blackness, the silver Throne was an island of calm matter. Not even aware he was doing it, Hanson stretched out a hand to touch it, to reassure himself with the cool feel of its solidity.

"Don't!" Boone said. "Only *I* can touch the throne—it's protected."

Hanson whipped his hand away. He had been intending, once Boone stopped talking, to urge him one more time not to do this thing. But now, overcome with futility, he knew he would not. What would be the use? A man like Boone, smart as he was, would never listen to somebody like *him*. And why *should* he? He was nothing much in the brains department, he knew it—never had been. Look at the mess he'd made of his life, look at how, all the way along the line, it had been someone *else*—Gossard, Willis, Boone—who had saved him from the consequences of his own stupid, blundering actions. Without them, he never would have made it. Without them, he never would have been standing here in the first place, way up here above the City of God, at the place where all the power of Heaven could be commanded. Without them, he'd be a pile of weathering bones somewhere, already stripped of flesh, already forgotten.

Hanson felt himself flushing with shame, suffused with a dull, ponderous embarrassment that seemed to turn his limbs to lead, congeal him solid where he stood, incapable of speech or action. He was a proud man—pride was what had gotten him into all this in the *first* place, after all. That is, he was a proud man when he had something to be proud *about*... but it seemed like he hadn't had that for a very long time. Certainly there was nothing to be proud about now, even though he was standing where no man had stood for who knew how many thousands of years. He'd gotten here in the first place through sheer blind blundering luck, and by taking advantage of the sharper wits of other men, and now that he was *here*, he really only half understood the situation, or what Boone was proposing to do, or the risks involved, or the rewards that might be gleaned. Even standing here before the Throne of God, even with all the strange and wondrous things that he'd been through, he hadn't been changed or elevated or ennobled—he was still just the common working slob he'd always been. Just a dumb ox. So why should he interfere? What right did *he* have to an opinion?

Keep your mouth shut, then, ox, he told himself bitterly. *Let the smart men decide how to run the world. Just as you always have.*

But, even with all of that running in his head, he couldn't help but feel a chill slice through him when Boone stepped up to the Throne. His mouth had gone dry with fear, and, when Boone reached forth a hand and actually *touched* the Throne, lightly, caressingly, Hanson felt the small hairs along his spine and on the back of his neck stir and stand up, one by one by one.

"I still don't think you should do this," Hanson said, in spite of himself, unable to keep the terror out of his voice.

"Don't worry," Boone said distractedly. "It's perfectly safe—for *me*." For a long still moment, he made no sound, and then he shook himself, gathering all his will and purpose. "Well," said Boone. "Here it is, then, the moment when History turns, when Mankind's destiny awakes from its long slumber!" He hovered over the Throne a moment, unable to work up the nerve to sit down and unwilling to retreat. "Now!"

He sat.

Grinning nervously, Boone gripped the armrests of the Throne. He took a deep breath. "This is a historic moment," he told Hanson. "Impress it on your memory. Forget nothing!"

Then he nodded to Cicero. "I am ready."

"As you will."

Five long needles of light converged upon Boone, piercing his skull.

"Ah!" he cried.

He stiffened, rising up slightly, and was silent.

For a long time, the little man sat wordlessly, staring straight ahead of himself, so far as Hanson could determine, into nothing. "Boone . . ." He reached out a tentative hand, and then, as Boone's wild eyes flicked in his direction, withdrew it. "Are you all right?"

Boone said nothing.

To Cicero, Hanson repeated, "Is he all right?"

"That is a difficult question to answer simply."

Abruptly Boone raised a hand. "Watch *this*!" The shifting blackness surrounding them transformed itself, so that they were staring across great reaches of the City of God. He pointed past a range of fang-thin pyramids (or maybe they were patterned neon stalagmites, high as skyscrapers—there was no way for Hanson to tell) to a park-like region where a flock of flamingos clustered like great masses of scarlet flowers at the edge of a shallow lake. Then he made his hand into a fist.

At Boone's gesture, the lake exploded upward. Water shot skyward, and, geysering, froze into a hollow latticework tube of ice that twisted and glittered wildly in the sun. Through the mist thrown out by the fantastic exchange of temperatures, Hanson saw the charred bodies of the flamingos falling like cinders.

"Do you know how much energy it took to do that? Fabulous amounts! More energy than was deployed by one of the nuclear weapons of antiquity. Oh, I wish you had the math to understand! It would stagger you to work out the figures!"

Staring at the blue-ice spire, all twisty and interwoven angles through a fog so dazzlingly bright he winced to look upon it, Hanson felt his mouth go dry. He swallowed hard and said, "What—what's it for?"

"*For?*" Boone laughed like a child. "For no reason at all! For the joy of the thing! Because I *felt* like it. I made it, and I can unmake it, if I wish, just like—that!"

He snapped his fingers.

The construction shattered. And even as the great shards were falling, Boone gestured again, the darkness re-forming around them, so that they were snug in the tiny room again.

"Now," Boone said, suddenly businesslike. "We must make plans. First, the Wall will have to come down. No question about that. But those who wish to benefit from my accomplishment must be brought to heel. I *know* them, you see. Oh, yes, I know their type! They will brush us aside with a pat on the head and a warning not to meddle, if they can; force is their all. They must be taught *respect*." He closed his eyes, thinking. "An object lesson, perhaps?" Then, offhandedly, "You can have my old rooms if you wish, Hanson. I think they'd suit you."

"You're . . . you're planning to live *here*?" Hanson said in horrified disbelief, staring about at the formless, crawling void that surrounded them.

Boone's eyes snapped open. "What? Of *course* I am! This room is the nexus, the focal point—anything I want can be brought to me here. Food. Books." With an oddly defiant toss of his head, he added, "Women."

Hanson twisted his mouth sourly. He understood well enough what was going on here, for he'd seen it happen before. Dumb as he might be, he wasn't so stupid he couldn't smell shit when somebody pushed his nose into it. Boone was turning himself into a *boss*. Seemed you couldn't get rid of them. Kill all the bosses, and the quiet guy who'd worked alongside you all his life and never once did anybody dirt would step forward to fill the vacancy and become a boss himself, and next thing you knew you were eating dust at *his* feet, right back where you'd always been. Nothing ever changed; it seemed like nothing ever really *could* change. He clenched and unclenched his fists in helpless and baffled anger.

"First, though—the Wall." Boone lifted his arms grandly.

The blackness before him bulged.

"What—?" Boone began.

A fierce and armless man strode up to the Throne, as stern and beautiful as an angel. His robes were afire, burning continuously without being destroyed. The smell of roasting flesh was nauseating. He frowned down upon Boone with blinded eyes whose sockets were encrusted with dried blood.

"My proud brother," the phantom said. "You have returned."

Boone's eyes widened in astonishment for the briefest of instants, then narrowed again, shrewdly. "I'm not your brother."

"You are a Renunciate. It is the same thing."

"I don't know what that means."

"It means you are human," Cicero said mildly, "of the race which built the City, but one of those who, given the opportunity to enter it, turned away."

Carefully, Boone said, "I am a Utopian—a citizen. You cannot question my authority." He slapped his chest. "I hold the key within me."

"You are no citizen!" The phantom pointed sternly at

Hanson. "*He* is a citizen. *He* holds the key to the City within him. You are allowed in the City only as his property. But even as his property, you have gone too far!"

It was the briefest of looks Boone threw Hanson, but one that spoke eloquently of hurt and betrayal, a look that pierced Hanson to the core of his being, that made him want to throw up his hands and protest his innocence. I didn't mean to do it, he wanted to cry. The key left you for me when you died. It wasn't *my* idea! If I'd known it was important—

But Boone, ever pragmatic, had already turned back to argue with his opponent. "Damnit, you can't condemn me for something I never *did*. I'm not one of your ancient enemies. Those who refused to enter the City with you are dead long ages ago. *I* didn't make that decision. I would have chosen differently."

"No matter! You are a Renunciate. The sin is in the seed. Time cannot expunge it. Your kind shirked the peril, the challenge, the transforming glory and horror, and for what purpose? In order to cling to your humanity! Your betrayal is not forgotten and can never be forgiven. It is too late for regrets."

"Listen!" Boone cried. "Those issues that divided your kind and mine are long dead. Yes, we were separated—let now the two streams reunite! It's time we were reconciled."

A short, angry slash of the head. "No!" The phantom's face was dark as thunder. "Too late, too late!"

"It's never too late!"

"It was *always* too late for you." Now the flames blazed hotter, so that the apparition became almost painfully bright, dazzling and terrible. "Look—see the price we paid for perfection!"

Briefly, Hanson saw the raw and bleeding wound where the man's genitals had been. He turned his head away, sickened.

"I tore off those parts with my own teeth and, oh, how I savored the pain of it! Could *you* have done as much?"

Boone could not speak.

The phantom smiled disdainfully as the flames burned low again. "I thought not. You came here seeking power and knowledge. Very well. Drink deep of both. Learn what we learned!"

Boone screamed.

It hurt the eye to look at him. He seemed to be vibrating; a kind of still motion possessed him, as if he were simultaneously shooting rapidly upward in the air and descending with equal speed into the ground. And yet he went nowhere. Boone's body had taken on the blurriness of extreme speed, a sort of translucence with nothing visible behind it. His face tensed, stretched, lengthened like cold taffy relentlessly pulled. His mouth stayed open, stretched to its extreme.

He screamed.

He screamed, and the scream went on and on, independent of the air in his lungs, endless, eternal, a condition of existence, a cry of pain and fear that stretched from the beginning of time to its end, like the shrill note of a violin string endlessly stroked, always on the verge of snapping and yet continuing, impossibly continuing. It simply *was.*

Hanson seized Cicero by the shoulders and shook him. "We'll leave!" he cried. "Tell *him,*" pointing to the phantom, "to let Boone go, and we'll leave. Tell him!"

"He cannot be reasoned with. Despite his appearance, despite his words, he is not a citizen. He is only a security function."

Hanson spun away, reaching for Boone, but Cicero stopped his hand. Slight though he was, Cicero was impossibly strong; Hanson, for all his muscle and bulk, could not free himself from his grip. "It would be extremely dangerous to touch him. It might kill you."

"You!" Hanson shouted to the phantom. "*You* can stop this!"

The phantom turned his sightless frown upon Hanson, but said nothing.

Now the air about Boone was streaking, congealing

into vertical strings of shattered light, greenish, as if the vibrations from the Throne were threatening the structure and nature of space about it. Boone hung agonized at the very center of this twisting chaos. His eyes were wide with pain, but sane. Unbearably sane.

His scream went on and on, unendurable.

"Cicero!" Hanson cried again. "He's dying!"

"No. He is suffering, but he will not die. He will not be *allowed* to die. He will wait here as a warning to all who would aspire beyond their state. The years will pass, and then the decades, and then the centuries. To him, the agony will be eternal."

"Get him off, damn you!"

"He is beyond rescue. The security function is implacable and absolute. A Renunciate has sat upon the Throne—he must be punished."

As if in a dream, Hanson felt his hands go to his belt. His gun was still there—the gun he had retained simply because it was the only thing besides Boone that he had brought with him to the City of God, the only thing he possessed that was undeniably his own.

He pulled it out.

This was not him acting; it was his body, obeying no conscious impulse of his own, but only the implacable logic of Boone's unending scream. Hanson watched, horrified, from a place behind his eyes as the gun swam into view. He expected Cicero to step forward to stop him. He expected the guardian function to confront him.

Neither did.

Awkwardly he slid the safety to off. He cocked back the heavy hammer. He raised the muzzle toward the blind-eyed guardian brooding over Boone's suffering. But when he did, the guardian turned upon him so unconcerned and disdainful an expression that Hanson knew without being told that it was useless, that mere bullets could not stop so powerful a being.

Stepping close to the Throne he raised the gun in both hands, so that it pointed right at the center of Boone's face, at a spot directly between the man's eyes. The agonized eyes that did not look at the gun but right through it, as if it hardly existed and certainly didn't matter, boring into Boone's eyes and pleading as clearly as words ever did:

Kill me.

I can't, he thought, even as his finger clenched around the trigger, squeezing it tight, fighting the balky mechanism of its action, a simple movement that was taking forever it seemed, impossible that it could go on so long, as if time had frozen to a gelid flurry, slowed, solidified, and then—finally—stopped.

The gun fired, with an appalling explosion of sound so loud it seemed to shatter Hanson's ears.

All in an instant, Hanson's hands went flying up and back, the recoil spinning the revolver itself through the air and sending it clattering across the floor. Boone's head slammed back into the Throne and bounced forward again. Flecks of blood and gore were everywhere, tiny droplets landing on Hanson's knuckles, his shirt front, his face. Boone's body pitched forward and fell heavily to the floor, facedown, as limp as a sack of laundry.

Silence.

The guardian turned to Hanson.

"You may assume control of the node now, if you wish."

Hanson raised his head, heavy with guilt, wordless with disbelief.

"It's true," Cicero said. "There's no danger to you. I know you believe yourself to be a Renunciate, but by testimony of the key you carry within yourself, you are not. You are a citizen. All functions must respect you. The security function would never offer you harm, not even to save the City itself."

Hanson shook his head bullishly, a rejection not so much of any specific words or actions as of everything: Boone's death, the raid on the brigand camp, his flight from Orange, the Pit, his childhood, his birth, *everything.*

With a respectful nod, the security function stepped backward, dissolving into blackness.

"Shall I clear this away?" Cicero indicated Boone's body.

Appalled, Hanson opened his mouth to say who knew what, and then caught control of himself and closed it again. Cicero didn't know any better—he was only a function. He wasn't real. Hanson slumped, closing his eyes. "Yes," he said. "Yes. Take it away, bury it."

"And this?"

Cicero held up the gun.

"Bury it along with him."

Then, because Boone had after all been a man of the cloth, he added, "Raise a stone or a sun-cross or something over it. Something appropriate." It was a hell of a thing for a man to die so far from home. A hell of a thing to pass unnoticed and unremarked by anyone you ever knew.

He stood waiting while Cicero picked up the body in his arms, stepped into darkness, and returned unencumbered. Then he said, "Let's get out of here."

Cicero led him to the stairwell. When he looked down it, he threw up.

~

What Hanson needed now, more than anything, was sleep. He was still standing, and that was all. Months might have gone by for Boone and Cicero, but for him, Hanson, by the clock of his heart, it had only been three days since he'd had his shoveling contest with the New Man back in the Pit in Orange. In fact, this was *still* the third evening, as far as he was concerned, although enough had happened in those three days to make it seem like a lifetime had passed, and in all that time he'd only had a fitful nap here and there, not really a decent night's sleep since leaving Orange. He was tired enough to make him believe that he had been awake and on his feet for every second of those eight months that Boone claimed had passed. Every cell in his body yearned for nothingness, darkness, oblivion.

At his direction, Cicero led him back to the spider-legged houses and into Boone's bedroom. It was spare and almost empty, with a small rectangular pad in its center, not much different from a working-class man's futon back in Orange. "Lie here," Cicero said, "and you will be refreshed."

With a nod, Hanson lay down on the pad. It was of an almost neutral texture, neither soft nor hard, just yielding enough to avoid discomfort, a trifle cool to the touch at first and then warm. He closed his eyes.

Five minutes later he opened them again.

He was wide awake.

Lying on the pad had refreshed his body, cleansed it

of fatigue poisons, and returned it to peak strength and vigor. Physically he was in terrific shape. Mentally, however, he felt the same as before—wasted, blasted, sick to the very pit of his being with the mere fact of existence.

He sat up, alert, unblinking, and knew then with an awful clarity that he was never going to be able to make any kind of life for himself here, that Heaven was simply not for the likes of him. He didn't know where home was for him anymore—perhaps there *was* no home for him anymore. But, wherever it was, it wasn't *here*.

He stood.

He walked out to the balcony.

He walked back in.

He walked back out.

Finally, there was no help for it. He was beyond evasions now.

Without looking at Cicero, he said, "Take me to the Throne of God."

~

No trace of Boone's violent end remained. Every least particle of blood had been cleaned away in his absence. The room was as sterile and empty as if no one had walked here for a thousand years. Or as if no one ever *had* walked here, since the first recorded tick of time.

Hanson sat gingerly down on the Throne, his body tensed and aching to leap up and away from its cold electric touch. He felt a surge of icy terror, but fought it down. This was the one moment in his life when he had a chance to actually *change* things, probably the one moment in the lives of all the hundreds of ancestors who'd striven and fought and toiled to produce him in the first place, who had lived their lives and broken their hearts and died without ever encountering a single moment where anything they did had even the remotest chance of effecting a real change in the world. This was the only chance any of them would *ever* have, even if he went back to the human world and had a dozen children and they lived a thousand generations more. This was the one chance for all of them, that chain of lives stretching back into the distant past and ahead into the unimaginable future. This one moment, here and now. He had to give it his best shot, and hope that things would work out all right. He didn't really know what he was doing, or what the consequences of it might be, but he knew he had to *try*. Perhaps it had been no different for God Himself, in the Beginning, when He'd set out to create the world.

He clutched the Throne's arms. "Show me where we are."

Cicero gestured, and the tower, walls and stairs and ceiling alike, became transparent.

Hanson stared over the City to the Wall, and over it as well, as if from a height even greater than the tower's: stared upon a landscape rendered toylike by distance, like a cunningly crafted panorama or three-dimensional map, but one in which things moved and changed position, as in the image cast by a *camera obscura* (one of which he'd seen in the Courthouse in Orange, as a boy) so that you could see horses and transports moving on the roads, and people working in the fields, and cows wandering as they grazed, and trees swaying in the wind. Through some post-Utopian magic, it seemed like he could see everything at once, see it all clearly and distinctly, no matter how far away it was, his whole old world laid out at his feet. First there were the Utopian ruins overgrown in calamity weed and scrub oak; somewhere down there was the clearing in which he'd met Boone. Then the road up which the transport had come so very long ago, leading back to the ancient highway that stretched back to the south, past the SI garrisons and gypsy camps, the tiny crossroads towns, the vast glinting silver snake of the river, the high iron bridge over the Hudson, and on to the patchwork of hardscrabble farms beyond, which clung precariously to a series of gently rolling hills like the folds of a carelessly thrown quilt. Then, finally, by the horizon, a low gray smear of buildings where Orange was. Leaning forward, looking closer, he could make out the fetid streets of the Bog, rising up into Blackstone (he almost thought he could see the window of his old apartment, where he had lived with Becky for so many bittersweet years), and then up into the Swank, tidy tree-lined squares surrounded by fine old brick-and-iron buildings. He could see the rusty-orange Courthouse dome, one of the few specks of color in a sea of brown wood and gray brick, and imagined that if he could somehow see *within* the dome itself he would see himself as a small child staring fascinated at the table where the image from the *camera obscura* shifted and glittered, as if the Utopian optics through which he was looking could somehow let him see back through time as well as off through space (as who knew if they could *not*?) . . . And then, raising his eyes, up the slopes of Industry Hill to the highest point in Orange, he saw at last the massive ugly bulk of the State Factory, where he had slaved away the best days of his life, where he had poured out his youth like water onto thirsty ground. If he leaned forward a bit more, he could see the lip of the Pit itself, and tiny figures moving on it, shoveling, turning away to dump their coal onto the pile, turning back to shovel again, bending and straightening, their tiny matchstick arms and legs scissoring, and perhaps one of them was Gossard, or the New Man, or—recalling his fancy of a moment before—perhaps even Hanson himself, staring at the Wall of the City of God as he shoveled, thinking all the while about God staring back at him with a huge watery eye, tall as the sky.

Something caught in Hanson's throat, and he blinked back sudden tears. No one knew better than he not to romanticize the world stretched out there below, no one knew better than he the miseries and brutalities it contained, the sickness and the poverty and the filth, the tyranny and murder. From up here, you couldn't see the crooked politics and institutionalized cruelties that were housed beneath the Courthouse dome that looked so picturesque and attractive. From up here, you saw only the pastoral beauty of the fields and the patchwork farms; you didn't see the grotesquely mutated animals and the cows with cancerous running sores and the "sour spots" in the fields, places too thoroughly drenched in ancient chemical poisons for anything to ever grow there again for millennia to come. Hanson *knew* all that, none knew it better.

And yet, even so, he was homesick.

He wanted to go home, wherever home was. Maybe not back to Orange, necessarily, but *home*. Back to the human world. Back where he belonged. Back to where children went fishing in the summertime and women leaned out of windows to catch a breath of air at evening, back to where cows grazed and people drank beer and laughed, back to where folks fell in love and had babies and grew old and died. Away from the inhuman, unchanging, cruel and incomprehensible alien splendor of *this* place.

"All that you can see, from here to the Wall," Cicero said, "is subject to your manipulation."

"How do I turn off the Wall?" Hanson asked gruffly.

"A twenty-mile section of it is under your control." Cicero waved a hand, indicating an arc reaching from horizon to horizon. "It can only be turned off by depriving this entire segment of the City of all higher functions. I do not advise it. If, however, that is what you wish to do, I will guide you through the protocol."

Hanson took a deep breath. "A'right," he said. "Let's do it."

He seized the chair's grips. The needles converged upon his skull.

To his surprise, it did not hurt. A glowing sensation radiated from the base of his spine, a pervasive warmth like the sun on a summer's afternoon. Lucid calm flooded his brain and he became aware of a thousand distant structures and devices, not as any kind of detailed knowledge but in much the same way he was aware of parts of his own body, ignorant of their inner workings but, with the slightest concentration, in control.

"What do I do now?"

"Make yourself aware of the Wall."

"A'right." He felt it now, within him, a glowing length of immaterial and impervious substance, reaching down three times farther into the bedrock than it extended above the ground. A thin, thin line reached even farther down, impossibly far, toward the core of the Earth, tapping energies incomprehensively greater than any he'd ever imagined. No phantom guardian appeared. No one challenged him. He did not ascend, descend, vibrate, scream. "What now?"

"Imagine a blue triangle. Within it, imagine a yellow circle. Now imagine that circle turning red."

He did.

Twenty miles of the Wall ceased to be.

~

It took Hanson three weeks to make his way out of Heaven to the mortal realm of York. He could still summon a cyclone by stepping on a silver pad, but he could not make it take him where he wanted to go. His first attempt carried him so far from the Wall that he was not tempted to try a second time, lest he lose himself so thoroughly he might never find his way out again.

Without Cicero, the City of God was unspeakably dangerous, capricious in unforeseeable ways. There was, so far as he could tell, no malice to it, but he was like a child lost in a steel mill; power was everywhere and he did not understand its purposes. The post-Utopians hadn't turned off any of their machines before they had gone away to wherever it was they had gone. And Cicero, who understood its workings, was gone too, canceled out along with the twenty miles of Wall, never mentioning that he was one of the "higher functions" that Hanson's command would send to oblivion. Hanson found he missed Cicero more than he did Boone, though the one was only a function and the other a real human being.

It was an awful thing to have to admit to himself.

He lived off rain water and what vermin he could catch, and he was often sick. It was a hellish time for him. But he kept going, determined that if he were going to die, he would at least make it to the Human Domain first. He would die on his own side of the Wall.

When finally, starving, Hanson crossed over into the borderlands of York, he was taken prisoner by a troop of State soldiers. They were out in force, establishing a string of camps where the Wall had been, digging ditches and earthwork ramparts, re-creating a crude parody of the Wall in order to control access to the City of God and its many presumed treasures. They were all of them badly spooked by this turn of events, fearful and uncertain of what the future would bring. An unquestioned chock of their reality had crumbled without warning, and if *that* could happen, then who was to say what else might or might not?

"Hands up!" the soldier shouted. He held his rifle too tensely. He was ungodly young, a child really. When Hanson obeyed, he eased hardly at all, remaining as taut as an overwound spring. "You're in bad trouble, mister."

"A'right," Hanson said. His head swam dizzily; he had to fight down a suicidal urge to caper and dance. But even in his weak and giddy state, he was particularly anxious not to be shot, not at this late date. "Y'caught me. You're the boss. I'll do whatever you say."

"Where'd you come from, anyway? How'd you get past the line?"

Line? "I came from the east." He gestured with his head, keeping his hands up as steady as he could. "Beyond where the Wall used to be."

The boy's eyes widened.

Two more soldiers came out of the woods. They both looked tough, but one looked mean as well.

"What you got?" one asked.

"This'n says he come from over the Wall."

"Yeah, right."

"So what do we do with him?"

The soldiers glanced one at another. There was an uneasy moment of balance when Hanson's fate could have gone any which way. The mean-looking soldier cocked up his mouth to one side, and, unslinging his rifle, said, "Too much fucking trouble to walk him back, if you ask *me* . . ."

The boyish soldier gaped at him, too horrified to interfere.

Talking quickly, saying any fool thing that came into his head, Hanson said, "Hey, any of you boys come from Orange? That's where I'm from, that's my neck of the woods. Maybe you got family back there? What are their names? Might be I know them." Crazy, nonsensical stuff he was saying, but it didn't matter—anything to establish contact.

The third soldier stared hard at him. Then—

"Fuck it," he said, and pushed the rifle barrel out of line, away from Hanson. The mean-looking one gave him an angry look, then turned his head to the side, spat, and re-slung his rifle.

The soldier who'd just saved Hanson's life looked tired. "We'll take him to camp. He can answer questions there."

They tied his hands behind his back and started down the road. Hanson went quietly. He knew his answers would not please their superior officers. Their questions would be all wrong. It didn't matter, though. He had done his part.

He had opened the City of God for them.

It might be some good would come of it. Anything was possible. He didn't intend to dwell on it, though. What they did with it was their concern, not his.

They walked on in silence for a while. Hanson felt weak and dizzy. After a mile or so, one of the soldiers struck a narc on his thigh, took a long drag to get it started, and stuck it in Hanson's mouth.

He mumbled his thanks. They wouldn't untie his hands, but after he'd sucked in, the young soldier who'd captured him took the narc out again so he could exhale.

The two older soldiers tended to keep a cautious distance from him, but the younger one hung at his side, not frightened any longer but curious, intrigued, obviously thinking over what Hanson had said earlier. Finally, he couldn't keep his questions in any longer. "You really been"—he made a gesture with his head—"back *there*?"

Hanson nodded wordlessly.

"Inside the City, I mean."

"*Ai.* S'pose I have."

"You ever seen . . . you know?"

The kid asked it in a hushed kind of way, the religious feelings of his childhood apparently not entirely dead yet, for the blasphemy of a ragged drifter like Hanson claiming to have come from the City of God was clearly thrilling and alarming to him. His buddies, skeptical, intrigued, moved a little closer to hear Hanson's answer.

"You mean God?" Hanson began to laugh. He couldn't help it. Stumbling to a halt, he managed to control himself, to still the painful laughter for just long enough to look into the boy's anxious face and say, "Fool! D'you mean to say you ain't heard yet? *God is dead!*"

He doubled over then, roaring with laughter. His eyes filled with tears, and still he couldn't stop. He laughed until he choked.

The soldiers waited until he could breathe again. Then they yanked him upright and double-checked his bonds.

They all four headed down the road.

6

THERE WAS A WINDOW in one wall of his cell. Without it, Hanson later thought, he might have gone insane.

It was a narrow slit window, open to the air but set with stout iron bars, a horizontal slash in the pale stone in the eastern wall of his cell, and although it let the cold wind in, and sometimes snow in winter, Hanson treasured it for the air and light it also let through into the gloomy darkness of his cell. The cell wall bulged inward slightly here, and with a little scrambling, it was possible to reach the window and hook your arms around the bars. Hanson would hang there for a long time, until the muscles in his big arms screamed in protest, relishing the cold wind on his face, drinking in the sight of trees and birds and low rolling hills, sometimes looking out toward the eastern horizon where, just out of sight, waited the shining immensity of the Wall of the City of God. Sometimes at night you could see its sullen glow lighting up the dark underbellies of the clouds.

When his arms could stand the strain no longer, he would slump back into the smothering, claustrophobic darkness of his cell, where he had a hard narrow cot, a few rough blankets, a pot to relieve himself in. They rarely came for him anymore, and most of his days and nights were spent alone, his meals—rough but substantial fare, bread that he could smell baking somewhere on the premises early in the morning, big hunks of new cheese, sometimes an unidentifiable piece of meat or a bit of fruit in the summer—shoved in through a slot in the iron-bound oaken door twice a day; at least they hadn't tried starving him yet, although they'd tried everything else. He rarely saw his captors anymore, although he could hear them passing in the corridor outside and had learned to recognize the individualities of their gaits, and to identify one guard by his habit of whistling jigs and cheerful little schottisches as he made his rounds. He hadn't seen any of the other prisoners for months, and never had seen much of them, although occasionally he could hear them screaming, or crying hopelessly in the night, and one evening someone had begun wailing "What *is* this place? I don't belong here! Let me out of here! Get me *out* of here!" over and over again for hours in a hideously wavering high-pitched voice, like a lost soul crying out from some deep pit of Hell, until finally it was cut off in mid-cry, followed by an ominous silence.

Hanson almost—almost—regretted that they didn't come to take him for questioning anymore.

His first day here, after soldiers quick-marched him from the City of God, which he had been caught coming out of, returning from a place no man had ever successfully entered in who knew how many hundreds or even thousands of years, they had dragged him to the warden's office. The warden had sat behind his scarred wooden desk and studied him dispassionately, as though he were some curious kind of bug.

"So, you claim to have been inside the City of God?" the warden asked, in a gravelly voice.

"Ai," Hanson said, and began to tell his story, but the warden, a pale, hulking fat man who reminded Hanson oddly of his long-lost friend Gossard, although a more brutish, corrupted Gossard with a hard face and harder eyes, surged to his feet and waved a fist the size of a ham at him. "Save your lies!" the warden screamed. "We'll get the truth out of you soon enough!" And when Hanson had started to protest, he'd swarmed into him, hitting him with his rock-hard ham fists, knocking Hanson to the ground, then kicking him twice in the ribs.

As Hanson looked up at him from the floor through a blaze of pain, the guards joined in on the fun, drawing hardwood truncheons from their belts and striking him over and over, smashing his rib cage when he held his arms before his face and then his face when he wrapped his arms about his torso. Two or three times he tried to rise to his feet and was clubbed back down. They worked steadily, methodically, and then, when Hanson honestly believed he was feeling as much pain as a human being *could* feel without actually dying, they stopped. There was a brief silence and then warm drops of water spattered over his face and body. Hanson's eyes were swollen shut by then, but he managed to open one just wide enough to see that the warden had unbuttoned his fly and taken out his thick ugly cock, and was calmly and methodically pissing all over him.

When he was done at last, the warden buttoned himself up again and made a flicking, dismissive gesture, like a man shooing a fly, and the guards had pulled Hanson up off the floor and dragged him through a maze of stone corridors for the first time to his cell, where they left him curled into a ball in the dirt, shuddering with nausea and shame, the rank smell of the other man's urine in his hair and nose, soaking his clothes.

The warden, whose name was Overton, later explained to Hanson, in one of those phases of interrogation where he would become ramblingly conversational, almost chatty, that this was a sound psychological technique, establishing dominance at once and breaking down any image the prisoner might have of himself as brave and noble and heroic by shaming and humiliating him. "No man can think of himself as heroic when his clothes are steaming with another man's piss, eh? Of course," Overton said, tapping a pale finger alongside his nose and winking, "the man who came before me would have raped you. Raped you and enjoyed it, too. Old Auxley was a vicious bastard. But the way I see it, there should always be something held in reserve. That's kinder in the long run, it heads off unwise actions. Just remember: no matter how bad things are, they can always get worse."

They left him alone in his cell for two days in his stiff, stinking clothes, without food or water, and on the third morning they dragged him to a windowless downstairs room whose walls were padded with blankets and straw. While Overton sat motionless and silent on a stool, the other guards "questioned" Hanson with practiced efficiency, making him run over his story again and again while they first beat him bloody with their fists, then put burning slivers under his fingernails, then seared his flesh with red-hot irons, then slowly crushed his foot in an iron vise. Hanson was not even remotely heroic through all this. He had been hurt before in his life, accidents at work, bar fights, had even been stabbed once, but nothing in his experience had prepared him for this kind of methodical torture, his body ripped open, his skin blistered and blackened, his bones crushed. He screamed his throat raw, cried, begged, and, toward the end, pleaded that he'd tell them anything they wanted to hear if they'd just *stop*. Throughout the procedure, Overton sat in complete silence, sometimes leaning forward intently, sometimes frowning slightly, as if that particular interrogation technique wasn't being carried out to his complete satisfaction.

Finally, Overton made another of his sharp, dismissive gestures, and the guards dragged Hanson back to his cell, where he huddled on his cot, moaning, oozing blood, shivering with pain and fever.

In the morning, he felt fine. His burns had healed, his skin had reknitted itself, his bruises had vanished, and his foot was once again uncrushed and whole.

The guards looked in on him and then went hurriedly away, and in a few moments, Overton was there, peering puzzledly at him, and then prodding Hanson's unmarked shoulder where his skin had been burnt and blackened with hot irons the day before. He gestured impatiently, and the guards dragged Hanson away to the basement room, where they did it all again.

This went on for days, the guards torturing Hanson while he begged them to just tell him what they wanted him to say and he'd say it, Hanson's wounds miraculously healing at night, leaving him hale enough to be tormented again the next day.

One day in the windowless room, Overton, who until

now had been silent during their sessions, greeted Hanson with an apologetic smile and said, "I'm sorry about this, Hanson, I really am. It's nothing personal. It's just my job." Two guards seized Hanson and wrestled him down into a chair, while another stretched Hanson's arm out across a thick wooden butcher's block that hadn't been there before that day. They strapped Hanson's arm in place, and one of the guards picked up an ax.

"For the love of God," Hanson said, his voice cracking shrilly in terror in the middle of the words, "don't *do* this!"

Overton shrugged philosophically. "Consider it a scientific experiment," he said, and then gestured to the guard, who stepped forward, hefted the ax, swung it aloft, and then cut Hanson's hand off with one crashing blow.

Hanson screamed. It actually didn't hurt as much initially as some of the other things that had been done to him in that room, but he could see blood fountaining from the stump of his wrist, and his throat squeezed shut with fear. Light rapidly drained from the world, the periphery of his vision going first, everything narrowing down to a cone. The room filled up with darkness.

The last thing he saw was Overton leaning forward to peer at him, and then laughing whimsically and saying, "Let's see him grow *that* back!"

He did. It took almost two days for Hanson's hand to

grow back, another day for him to recover full use of his fingers.

Overton came to Hanson's cell, stared at the regrown hand, and left without a word, looking frightened. The guards also gave him fearful looks out of the corners of their eyes, showing the whites, and backed out of the cell, closing the door behind him.

~

There were no more torture sessions after that. Two or three times a week, Hanson—who had by this point been allowed a change of clothes—would be "invited" to Overton's office, where Overton would be sitting at his desk, head bowed over some papers. "Sit down," he would always say. "I'll be right with you." As if they two had a professional relationship, as if Hanson were his client and had an appointment to be here, as if he were simply providing a service that Hanson required—as if the days Hanson had spent in the torture chamber had never happened at all. He would be placed in a straight-backed wooden chair in front of Overton's desk, sometimes given a cup of chicory or even a mug of applejack, and encouraged to "have a nice talk" with Overton, who wrote everything Hanson said down in a notebook in a surprisingly neat and even delicate hand. Hanson cooperated with this process as best he could, anxious to keep Overton in what Hanson thought of as "Good Overton" mode; he was already all too familiar with "Bad Overton." After a while, though, having gone over his experiences in the City of God—it seemed they believed now, belatedly, that he'd really been inside the Wall—in exhausting detail more than once, he ran short of things to say, and Overton filled the gap by rambling on about himself, becoming expansive and discursive, and not a little self-aggrandizing, boasting about his position and his prowess, telling Hanson all about the problems and tribulations of running a prison full of recalcitrant hard-core prisoners who didn't understand all the lengths he went to in order to *help* them. Hanson found this more than a little creepy, but it was better than being burned with red-hot irons, even if his flesh was going to heal the next day, so he did his best to play up and look interested and attentive.

The last time Overton had Hanson brought to his office, though, before Hanson had even had a chance to sit down, Overton had frowned and said, "I have asked for advice on your case. The responsibility has been passed on. There's nothing more I can do." He then gestured dismissively, impatiently, as if Hanson was wasting his valuable time by importuning him with unreasonable requests about inconsequential matters. The guards hustled Hanson away, back to his cell.

After that, he was left alone. They never came for him anymore, no one asked him any more questions. In fact, he barely saw another living soul from one week to the next, except when the guards came into his cell to empty his slop jar, keeping a wary, almost frightened eye on him while they did so, and refusing to speak.

He was left alone in his cell, only occasionally hearing another human voice far off somewhere in the corridors outside. He learned to relish and even long for the off-key whistling of the guard as he went by on the other side of the door, a sound other than his own breathing, and eventually learned which tunes the guard most liked to whistle. Once he started whistling the same jig that the guard was whistling as he passed, and the guard's whistling cut off with a frightened abruptness and didn't start up again for several days.

He lost track of time. Had months gone by, or years? Winter came, and left, and came again.

~

Hanson looked out his window. It was the only thing left to him, his lifeline to the world beyond his cell, and he drank in the bright, moving, multicolored normality that came in through it like a man desperately breathing through a hole in the ice.

He came to know every branch visible in every tree, the shape and size and colors of their leaves and berries, where every bird had its nest. He learned to identify the different kinds of birds by their calls, and even, through patient listening, came to gain some idea of what information those calls contained, whether it was "This is my tree!" or "I want a mate!" or "Look out for the fox!" There were marmoset-like little creatures living in the rocks at the near end of the field, and he watched avidly as they went about their daily dramas, squabbling over territory and mates, whistling shrill alarm calls and hiding from predators—or presumed predators, since Hanson never saw any—in amongst the rocks; one whole summer they tried doggedly to teach themselves how to light a fire, making piles of branches and dry tinder, breaking Hanson's heart by failing again and again and again. Occasionally, a bee or a fumblefoot would buzz by the window, sometimes even coming in through the bars to zip around inside the cell before finding their way back out again. One glorious day, a hawk struck a pigeon just outside the window, and carried it to a nearby stump to eat, tearing at the pigeon's breast and releasing a swirling cloud of torn white feathers as it fed that rose and danced on the wind, Hanson luxuriating in the motion—motion! A flurry of blessed activity and change in a static world! Something different!—like a man dying of thirst who's been offered cool water. Very occasionally, the highlight of the week, the memory of which he would cherish and turn over in his mind again and again until it was polished smooth, riders on horseback or a wagon would pass in the curve of the road visible at the far end of the meadow. Once, in the dog days of summer, heat hanging in the air as thick as honey, he saw a naked little boy driving a herd of bedraggled, ulcerated, two-headed goats before him. In the spring and fall, deer would sometimes come out of the deep woods near the marmoset rocks, some of them bearing glossy radiation scars from where they'd come in contact with one of the old "hot spots," and blink at him with their sad, liquid eyes. If he spoke to them, trying to coax them closer, or perhaps just to hear his own voice, they would vanish like ghosts.

There was a ruined wall in the middle distance, partway between him and the road, a tumbled fall of stone and crumbling brick marking the spot where some building had once stood. Halfway up the remains of the wall, there was a shallow horizontal ledge where windblown dirt had collected, and there a tree, one of the hardy kind that sprouts like weeds, had taken root and grown, clinging precariously to the side of the wall. Hanson became fascinated by this sickly little tree, perhaps because he could never decide whether it symbolized hope—life persisting against all odds, clinging to the thinnest possible margin to survive, but surviving nevertheless—or futility, since although it struggled to grow, it really had no place to grow *to,* was already stunted and yellowed by lack of nutrients, and sooner or later must wither and die. It struck Hanson forcefully that one of those things was the perfect metaphor for human life on Earth. But which one?

~

As he stared from his window, the world gradually changed, and not just with the changing of the seasons.

On a cold, cloudless night, clinging to the window bars, it was sometimes possible to watch the Bear or the Scorpion or other constellations rising over the edge of the Earth. He was watching, one night, when there arose an actinic purple glow on the northern horizon that sponged away the stars. From then on, the fizzing purple glow was always there, dimly visible even in the daylight if you shaded your eyes to look.

A few days later, a ragged wave of refugees came south down the road, grim, silent men and women carrying bindles and dragging sledges piled with household goods, herding both straggling children and straggling pigs and sheep along before them. For most of a day they streamed past, looking down or inward, not speaking, and then they were gone, around the bend in the road and out of sight.

Sometime later, there was a brief firefight down there at the bend of the road, small groups of men in unfamiliar uniforms blazing away at each other, some with guns, some with weird-looking implements that emitted flashes of light. Hanson clutched the bars of his window tight, reveling in the sudden flurry of action and drama, not stopping to worry that a stray bullet might hit him. Would it even kill him if it did? After a while, the firefight moved off into the woods, leaving bodies sprawled lifelessly across the road until someone from the prison with a mule and wagon came out and hauled them away. In retrospect, it occurred to Hanson to be ashamed that the killing down there had been nothing but a welcome diversion to him, a break in the numbing routine; they were men who had died down there, after all, spilling their blood and giving their lives to inadvertently provide his vicarious entertainment. Prison was changing him, wearing him thin, making him less human.

At night now, when the prison itself was quiet, he could hear strange booming noises off in the distance, ponderous and slow and very far away, like the footsteps of some unimaginably huge beast, and occasionally there were strange wailings and unearthly shriekings that put the hairs up on the back of his neck. Lights flared on the horizon, dimmed, flared again, pulsed rhythmically.

One moonless night, peering from his window, Hanson had seen a huge indistinct shape like an immense metal spider go by, momentarily occulting the stars as it passed, padding soundlessly up the road.

There were strange things abroad in the world now.

The world was changing, becoming an unfamiliar place, leaving him behind. He'd felt trapped, buried, in the State Factory in Orange, his life crushed beneath its smothering weight, compelled to recognize that his whole existence had been for nothing, that it had no point or reason at all. Once he had had dreams and a wife. Both were long dead. Even after he'd been forced to flee Orange and miraculously found his way through the Wall surrounding the City of God, possibly the first man ever to do so, how much credit could he take for that? The only extraordinary thing he'd ever done in his life—and that mostly against his will, from necessity, being driven by forces beyond his control and by the will of other, better men—had been to enter the City of God, and decline an opportunity to assume godlike power . . . and, almost as an afterthought as he left, to shut off one section of the Wall. Was all this strangeness his fault, for having let men into the City of God, where they were not supposed to go?

If so, then the one moment of significance in his futile, meaningless life, for better or worse, was behind him now. From here on, it would make no difference that he'd ever been born.

It was clear that he'd never get out of here. It was clear that he'd die here, and be absorbed tracelessly into the dark river of anonymous and forgotten dead who stretched back to the very beginnings of humanity, most of them having lived and died without leaving so much as a mark on the slick, impervious surface of the world, nor any indication that they'd ever been there at all.

~

One morning in late winter or early spring, there were horses waiting impatiently in the forecourt, eight or ten of them, blowing steam from their noses and scraping with their hooves at the glittering hoarfrost that coated the cobblestones. Hanson could just see them from here, if he pressed his face out as far as it would go between the cold metal of the bars. Of the riders, there was no sign; they must have entered the prison. For no particular reason, he felt a thrill of unease—someone important must be visiting.

An hour or so later, he heard footsteps approach his cell door and stop in front of it, then the rattling of the lock as someone fumbled with it. He sat up on his cot, feeling an odd surge of mingled anxiety and anticipation.

The door swung open. The whistling guard stood there, accompanied by two of his fellows, all wearing truncheons at their belts. "On your feet, freak," the guard said.

They hustled him down the familiar corridor to Overton's office, but Overton wasn't there. Instead, a tall, almost painfully thin man sat behind Overton's desk, and unfolded himself to get to his feet as Hanson entered. He was expensively, almost foppishly, dressed, with lace at his sleeves and ruffles on his silk blouse, and wore thigh-high riding boots of gleaming black leather.

"Ah, Hanson," he said, his face breaking into what seemed to be a broad, genuinely good-spirited grin. "I'm very glad to meet you at last." It sounded like he really was. "I'm Salvatore Delgardo," he said. Then, without changing expression or taking his eyes off Hanson, he said to the guards standing close behind, "Hold him."

Two guards seized Hanson from either side, holding him fast.

Then, before Hanson had a chance to struggle or even react, Delgardo came forward around the desk, picked up a broad-bladed knife, and, with one swift motion, cut Hanson's throat.

Hanson tried to scream, but could only make a strangling noise. The world did a slow somersault. He didn't realize that he had fallen to the floor until he saw Delgardo standing over him. Delgardo had taken a cup from the desk, and now leaned close over Hanson and filled it with the blood that pumped from Hanson's throat, being fastidiously careful not to splash any blood on his shirt. As Hanson watched in horror and amazement, his eyes already dimming, Delgardo raised the cup of blood to him in salute, and then drank it down in a single gulp.

The last thing Hanson heard was Delgardo's cheerful voice saying, "Hanson, we're going to be the greatest of friends!"

~

Hanson awoke that night in his cell, and instinctively clutched at his throat, but the wound was gone. He lay motionless in the darkness for a long time, listening to voices rise and fall somewhere off in the depths of the prison, too far away to make out the words. A door slammed somewhere with iron finality. The full moon looked in between the bars of the window like a fat bone-white face.

~

In the morning, they came for him again. He was taken to a part of the prison he'd never seen before, what must be the guards' quarters, given water and coarse potash soap to wash with and new clothes, plain but sturdy, and had his hair cut short by a scowling, sour-smelling old woman—the first woman Hanson had seen, he realized, in however many years he had wasted away in his cell. Then they took him back out through the corridors to Overton's office—or he supposed it was Delgardo's office now. Overton seemed to be gone.

Delgardo was behind the desk, reading through a thick file of papers. He looked up, said, "Ah, Hanson! Come in, come in!" in a jovial tone, swept the papers into a sheaf and tamped them straight, then opened a drawer and made the papers disappear into it. He waited until Hanson, in response to his gesture, had sat down and the guards had left the room, then raised his hand portentously, with great significance, and stretched it out, palm first, toward Hanson. "I must thank you, my dear friend," he said, "for making me immortal." Hanson stared at him. "The first thing I did after they dragged you from the room," Delgardo continued, "was slice my own hand, right here across the palm. Sliced it wide open. And look!" He brandished the hand theatrically in Hanson's face. "The wound closed up! The wound is gone! I can't be hurt!"

"You can be hurt," Hanson said dully. "Believe me, you can."

Delgardo chuckled. "Perhaps," he said, "but it's going to be damn difficult to kill me. Just like you." He took the sheaf of papers out of the drawer again and flattened them on the desk, smoothing them lovingly with his long musician's fingers. "That fool Overton had it all written down, but couldn't ever *see* it. I'm surprised that oaf could even read! Whereas I have pored over every word again and again, for months, and it's all here, in Boone's explanations to you." He pointed a finger at Hanson dramatically. "Cicero pumped your blood full of little machines that keep you healthy and repair any damage to you." He was referring to events and people—well, Boone had been a person, anyway—from so long ago that Hanson had almost stopped believing in them. "By drinking your blood, I now have the same little machines within me! So I too am immortal!" He smiled broadly. "Once I read about your hand growing back, I knew what I had to do! Cut your throat!" He laughed good-naturedly.

Something deep inside Hanson told him that Delgardo was wrong; that he didn't understand a thing about what was inside of him, and possibly never *could* understand it. Delgardo was a savage recasting strange technologies into terms he could understand: magic and tiny machines. But he only said, through gritted teeth, "Suppose it didn't work? Suppose I'd died?"

Delgardo shrugged, as if that was a matter of little consequence. "That would have been too bad," he said indifferently. "Now, since you *didn't* die, however, we must go on to discuss other matters of great importance!"

He tidied up the sheaf of papers again, then stared portentously at Hanson for a number of long silent moments. "It's a funny thing," he said. And waited.

"What is, sir?" One of the first things Hanson had learned from Overton was to respond politely when Overton paused that way if he wanted to keep him in "Good Overton" mode. Sometimes it helped. Sometimes it made the session go more smoothly. Not always.

Delgardo's mouth curled up in a wry little smile, as if he was about to wink and impart a confidence. "The sovereign Government of the State of York has sent hundreds of men into the City of God, and, funny thing, sooner or later they all die! They die or else they're . . . changed. Not a one of them has lasted a fraction as long as you did. Not a one of them has been able to close down any other sections of the Wall, other than the one you closed. Why do you imagine that is?"

"I've told you everything I know," Hanson said.

"I'm sure you have," Delgardo said in a way that indicated he didn't believe any such thing. "But here's the odd part. We give them all the information we've learned from you and from others who've gone into the City, but it doesn't seem to do them any good. We're still restricted to that one section of the City that was opened when you left it, and no one can go deep into it or find a way shut down the rest of the Wall. Most of the City, vast areas, are still unreachable! And these are tough, capable men. Trained soldiers. Clever young men. Frankly, much cleverer and tougher and more capable than *you* ever were, as far as I can tell. We send them out, and, sooner or later, they don't come back. We don't make any progress at all. Now isn't that funny?"

Hanson didn't say anything.

Delgardo stared at him. "Has anybody told you we're at war?"

Startled, Hanson said, "No, sir. I've heard no news in here. The guards never talk to me, and Overton never talked about what was happening on the outside." The firefight he'd seen on the road had been a hint, of course—but nothing so definite as what he'd just heard; it could have been a skirmish with bandits or outlaw gangs like the one he'd once briefly joined himself. Nobody had claimed that the war had actually *begun*. "Is it the South?"

Delgardo looked at him.

"That . . . that we're fighting with, I mean." Then, as the

silence grew uncomfortably long, he added, "Sir."

Now Delgardo smiled sadly in a way that made Hanson's blood run cold with fear. "Oh, Carl, Carl, Carl," he said. "What difference can it possibly make to *you*, of all people?" His voice took on a reminiscent tone. "Remember when you were in that dark place with the catwomen? Remember how frightened you were, how you thought then that you might die, and you didn't even know why?" Hanson felt the hair on his arms prickle with alarm. He really *had* read Hanson's testimony closely, and with unsettling comprehension and attention to detail. This was someone much more intelligent than Overton, and, as a result, probably much more dangerous. "This war is something like that. The *who* and *why* of it don't matter, only what might happen to us all as a result." He leaned forward, as if he'd just made a telling argument and was going to follow up on it. "This friend of yours, the one you call Cicero . . ."

"He wasn't a real person, I don't think. He said he was a function."

"Yes, yes, you've said that already. The question is, why hasn't anybody *else* seen him? So many have gone in, and of those who have come back out, not one has reported anything like him."

"It was Boone that he talked to," Hanson said. He was treading on dangerous ground here, perilously close to the tiny knot of information he had managed to withhold from the interrogators—that, through Cicero, who was willing to obey him because he held the key within him, he was able to control the City of God, at least to some extent. It was not a power he wanted, he had turned his back on it and walked away. It was not a power anybody should have. It was certainly not a power he wanted *Delgardo* to have. "Boone gave him orders. He wouldn't obey me."

"Yet he rescued you that time. With the cats. Why is that?"

"I . . . I dunno. Maybe Boone told him to."

"And why would Boone do that?"

"I dunno. Boone liked me. Boone was my friend."

"You know more than you're telling," Delgardo said. He was silent for so long then, staring at Hanson, that, in spite of the desperateness of his situation, Hanson began to get bored and started to fidget.

"I tell you what, my dear old friend," Delgardo said at long last. "I believe that you're concealing vital information in a time of war. Now, for that, I could send you back to the torture chamber and try to rip the truth out of you. But instead I'll make you a generous offer." He held up a long pale finger. "You'll come back to the City of God with us, with me and a small party of picked men. There you'll guide us around, show us everything you know, and we'll see if maybe this Cicero of yours will come out for you. If he does come out and talk to you again, as he hasn't done for anyone else, maybe we can get him to open the rest of the City up for exploration, and we can find some juicy new piece of Utopian technology that will make a decisive difference in the war, unlike the ones we've already exploited." He smiled brightly at Hanson. "If you do that, then the treason you've committed will be forgiven and forgotten, all your crimes will be forgiven and forgotten, even the murder of Oristano"—Hanson looked up in surprise; he knew about that too?—"back in Orange, and we'll let you go free. Free! Yes, a generous offer, I know, considering the magnitude of your crimes, but extraordinary times call for extraordinary measures!" He beamed at Hanson, as if he expected him to gush with gratitude. "So, what do you say?"

At the thought of returning to the City of God, of plunging again into those shining, alien, bewildering, incomprehensible spaces, Hanson felt such a wave of terror that the blood drained from behind his eyes and he almost passed out. He feared the torture chamber, yes, but he feared that more, feared it on a deep instinctual level that was almost cellular, that filled him with such dread that he thought his lungs would stop working.

"I—can't," he managed to choke out at last, not daring to look at Delgardo. "I can't ever go back there! Don't ask me to! You don't know, you don't know what it's like! I can't do it, I can't go back there again! I just—can't."

Delgardo smiled sadly. "That was the wrong answer," he said, and rapped sharply on his desk. The whistling guard came in and hit Hanson behind his ear with a truncheon, and they dragged him away, only partially conscious, and locked him back in his cell again in the dark. He could hear Delgardo sighing regretfully behind him as he went.

Early the next morning, just after dawn, the guards filed silently into Hanson's cell and shoved a leather bag over his head and down over his chest. Then they shackled his hands behind his back. Without a word being spoken, they dragged him from his cell and off through the long maze of corridors, Hanson stumbling blindly along, struggling to breathe through the thick, stifling enclosure of the leather bag, struggling to fight back the rising tide of panic.

He was about to die. It seemed impossible that he could still care after all he'd already been through. But he did.

Could they kill him? Hanson didn't know, but they could certainly try—cut him completely to pieces maybe, or douse him with oil and set him on fire. There must be limits to his "immortality." Maybe they'd succeed in killing him, maybe not, but he didn't want to find out which it was. Suppose he was still alive after they'd cut him to bits, or burned him black in the fire? Suppose he lived like that forever, in unending agony? Even if it did succeed in killing him, just the thought of going through that kind of ordeal, enduring that kind of pain, far, far worse than anything he'd suffered to date, loosened his bowels and made them rumble.

At last they came to a stop. Hanson waited inside the smothering darkness of the bag for several endless moments, choking and gasping, and then the bag was yanked abruptly from his head.

They were outside the prison, on the stone steps that led down to the forecourt. Cool air touched his face in the instant that the leather hood was whisked away, and light filled Hanson's eyes. He stood blinking, feeling wind ruffle his hair, feeling sunlight on his skin, smelling the turned-earth smell as the world began to warm toward spring. There were green buds just beginning on the trees, and birds were singing. Involuntarily, Hanson began to cry. He knew that he should be ashamed of the tears running down his cheeks, ashamed at having been unmanned, but he couldn't stop himself.

At his elbow, Delgardo said, "Maybe I can't kill you, although we could make it very unpleasant for you trying, but Hanson, my boy, we can certainly *keep* you here. Keep you here, and lock you away in the deepest dungeon so that you never see the sun again, ever, or feel the wind on your face. Keep you here forever, or as long as it takes you to finally die, even if it's a hundred years. Even if it's a thousand years! A thousand years of darkness and misery! Of nothingness! Locked away from the world! Or—" He paused. "—you can be brave enough to go back to the City of God, no matter how terrible a place it is, and be *free*. Free! Be given the world again! Be alive and out and about in the world again! Part of life, not sunk in darkness and enclosure, but really and truly *living* again!"

He lowered his voice to a whisper, his breath a soft tickle in Hanson's ear. "I can undo the shackles and you can walk down these steps and be part of the world again. Or you can turn around and go back inside. Back to four stone walls and a darkness that never ends. The choice is yours."

Hanson looked out across the meadow, watching the breeze ruffle the tall grass. He could see his tree from here, the one growing in a cramped niche on the side of a ruined wall, and it seemed to him that no matter how stunted and sickly it was, it was still alive, still surviving, and that therefore, as long as it did still live, there was still hope for it. And that the same applied to him, and maybe to the whole damned human race.

Or was he just rationalizing, taking the easy way out,

refusing to make the hard right choice? Taking instead a way that he and maybe the whole world would come to bitterly regret? Because they'd broken him, because he'd reached his limits and just couldn't take it anymore, be damned to the consequences?

If so, well . . . So be it, then.

"All right, Delgardo, you incredible bastard," Hanson said, "let's go back to the City."

7

THERE WERE TEN HEAVILY armed mounted soldiers, plus Delgardo. They had brought an extra horse for Hanson, and laughed openly at him when he failed at his first two attempts to mount it, sliding to the ground while the horse snorted and moved about uneasily, as if it didn't like his smell. At last, painfully, he hauled himself into the saddle. The beast rolled an eye back at him and snorted again, but then settled down resignedly. Hanson had only had a couple of occasions to ride a horse in his entire life, and he'd forgotten the strange feeling of all that breathing, moving muscle under him that he was somehow supposed to control; it took him a few tries to get the horse moving in the right direction, eliciting more laughter all around, but at last they set off.

It was strange, very strange, to be riding across the meadow he'd studied from his window for so long, watching the little marmoset-like creatures scatter and dive into their holes in the rocks to hide at their approach, and Hanson experienced a wave of dizziness and unreality that almost made him fall from his horse, and it took him a moment to convince himself that this wasn't a dream, that it was really happening, that he was *outside,* and let the world settle again around him.

At the bottom of the meadow, they turned onto the road where the firefight had happened, and which the refugees from some battle somewhere had streamed down, and he turned in his saddle to watch until the grim bulk of the prison disappeared from sight. As it did, he felt another wave of unreality, and then, the last thing he'd ever expected to feel, a surge of hope, and he prayed that he'd never see that place again in his life. The thought of returning and being interned again in its airless depths filled him with horror. He realized that Delgardo was right—better to take his chances with whatever destiny had in store for him in the City. Even if it killed him, maybe it would at least be a quick death. Better that than going back to where he'd rotted for so long.

As he became more comfortable with the unfamiliarity of riding, he began to pay less attention to controlling his mount and more attention to breathing in the world around him, an unbelievable luxury he'd almost forgotten during the time when all he could experience of life was a slit-window in a stone wall. A breeze had come up from the south, smelling of spring, the first wildflowers were opening to either side of the road, and there was a kind of tree growing in clusters here that he was unfamiliar with, leaves a bright vivid red, as though it was burning, flaming with life. Even the pungent smell of his horse's sweat was welcome.

He was still convinced that they were all headed for their deaths—but Death was not here *yet*; there was still time to enjoy a few more heartbeats, a few more breaths, luxuriate in the sultry breeze rich with the smell of life. Life, for however long it lasted, was its own reward, its own reason for being, and Hanson thought again about his poor stunted tree, trying somehow to grow in inhospitable soil in a niche in a ruined rock wall; if it could think, would it rather it had never existed, or would it be grateful for whatever time it had been given? Existence was the greatest gift imaginable. Maybe that was why life was so filled with misery and heartbreak—because something so valuable required the highest price imaginable, just so it could be properly appreciated.

As their party approached another stand of the flame-trees, they flushed a small herd of hoppers, who bounded across the road in front of them with prodigious leaps. Delgardo stood up in his stirrups, stretching his arms wide to either side in a flamboyant, look-at-me gesture, then drew a long-barreled pistol from a saddle holster and snapped off a seemingly casual and unaimed shot that nevertheless caught one of the hoppers in mid-leap and sent it crashing to the ground, where it twitched and gasped among the dust of the road. "Fresh meat tonight, boys!" he crowed, well-pleased with himself, and dispatched two of the soldiers to finish off the dying hopper, dress and quarter it, and store the hurriedly wrapped meat behind their saddles. While this was going on, Delgardo, still standing in his stirrups, grinning broadly, made his horse prance in a little circle, as though he were waiting for applause, and it didn't seem to bother him that none came.

He couldn't be more pleased with himself, Hanson thought, shaken out of his philosophical musings. He doesn't need anybody else to applaud for him, he'll do it for himself. Hanson had run across men like this a few times before, usually members of the aristocracy, with the unquestioned assumption of superiority that growing up rich gave you. With a chill, Hanson realized that Delgardo's ego was so vast and swollen that not only did he think he was the most important person in the world, expecting acknowledgment and admiration from everyone else for that fact, but he thought that he was the *only* person in the world, the only real person, with everyone and everything else reduced to the role of unimportant spear-carriers in the unique and miraculous drama of his life. Such people were dangerous. He'd already known that Delgardo was dangerous, of course—he'd cut his throat, after all, even if he wasn't really expecting Hanson to die—but now the realization set deeper in that Delgardo would sacrifice him, or anybody else, in a heartbeat if it enabled him to get what he wanted. He'd have to be very cautious with how he behaved toward Delgardo if he wanted to get out of this alive—but then, he realized, with a curious kind of relief, that really didn't matter. The City would kill them all anyway.

After an hour or so on the road, they turned east, toward the City of God.

~

The road leading to the City of God had been considerably widened since Hanson had seen it last. Back then, when he was marched to captivity, hands tied behind his back, it had been little more than a track in the forest. Now it was big enough to accommodate a constant flow of mule-drawn army wagons, those headed inward loaded with food and supplies, those outward mostly empty, though some few were heavily laden and those few covered with heavy canvas tarps and guarded by more armed soldiers than seemed necessary.

"The fewer questions you ask, the less you'll have to regret," Delgardo said when he caught Hanson staring at one of those wagons. But Hanson had known better than to ask questions out of simple curiosity for longer than he cared to remember. It was one of the first things that got beaten out of you in school. He simply looked away—away from the wagons, away from the guards, away from Delgardo's hard stare. He heard a snort of scornful amusement from the man as he did so, but he didn't rise to the bait.

A few miles later, from the top of a small rise, they got their first look at the Wall of the City of God. Hanson had seen it at a distance every day of his working life, as he slaved away up on an outdoor platform at the State Factory in Orange, and, to his sorrow, he had seen it close-up once before—but it was still a breathtaking sight, beautiful and terrible, so that his emotions snagged in his throat as he looked at it. The Wall, hundreds of feet high, stretched out of sight in either direction, extending more than five hundred miles from south to north. It glowed, smoldering with pinks and coral reds, and Hanson well remembered the heat it generated, like walking into a furnace if you got too close.

The shining immensity of the wall had a black gap in it, directly ahead, as if someone had knocked out a great beast's two bottom front teeth—marking the place where, long ago, Hanson had shut down that section of the Wall, allowing humans entry to the City of God beyond.

Hanson had a wild moment of panic where he considered turning his horse around and making a break for it, galloping as fast as he could go—but it was hopeless. Delgardo would bring him down as easily as he had the hopper, or some of the other, much more experienced horsemen would catch up with him. Reluctantly, he followed the others down the hill toward the City, his fear growing as the Wall rose higher and higher above them.

Since he'd last been here, an Army encampment had been built alongside the gap in the Wall, hundreds of tents clustered close around a few plain, obviously hastily slapped-together wooden buildings. As they rode up, Hanson saw detachments of soldiers working to raise a wooden palisade to replace the section of Wall that had been taken down. A second palisade surrounded the camp. Nearby was a cemetery and there were soldiers working there too, digging graves for canvas-wrapped corpses and filling them in again. Delgardo noticed him looking and said, "That's right, Hanson. There was a big incursion from the South only three days ago, soldiers trying to drive us out and take over control of the City. There was a pitched battle in which hundreds died on either side. These are the poor bastards who lingered for a while in the hospital tents. See what you've wrought, eh? If you'd never opened up the City of God, those men wouldn't have died." He smiled gently at the graves. "And a lot more men are going to die in the future! All because of you." He sounded oddly pleased at the prospect. Hanson tightened his jaw, but said nothing.

In the camp, they surrendered their mounts to the quartermaster. Hanson learned that horses went mad with fear if you tried to take them into the City, and refused to go no matter how much you whipped them, even if you whipped them to death. They'd have to walk from here on. Nor were horses the only ones afflicted. When the soldiers stayed too long in the City, they had horrible dreams which grew worse with every passing night until they refused to sleep for fear of what they would see, grew rebellious and hard to command, and even—some of them—went mad. So, after a few abortive attempts to build a base inside the Wall resulted in an untold number of deaths and suicides and one near-mutiny, the officers had given in and raised the camp outside, at a respectful distance from the City of God, and, they hoped, from the malign influences it seemed to radiate.

While their sergeant—a man with the unlikely name of Barker, usually appropriate enough for a sergeant, although Barker was a quiet man with tired, pouched eyes that had seen too much and knew that they were going to see more—went to arrange tents for them, they sat around in a rest area. Hanson was struck by what a glum and dispirited camp it was, lacking the horseplay and jocular shouted insults that would usually characterize a bunch of off-duty soldiers with nothing to do but wait for the mess hall to open as dusk came on.

Once, when Hanson was a boy, he saw a "gorilla," although it was more likely to have actually been one of those half-human hybrids that the ramshackle little nations to the west kept trying to use as soldiers. It was in a cage on a wagon in a pathetic little carnival that had passed through town, and all the children had come running out to jeer at it and poke at it with sticks between the bars. The ape had ignored them all, enduring everything, simply sitting and staring at nothing.

That was how the soldiers sat, empty-eyed and uncaring, not looking at anything, nor so far as could be determined thinking anything either. Marshaling their strength for the next battle.

It occurred to Hanson to wonder if York was losing this war. Then it occurred to him to wonder if there even *was* such a nation as the State of York anymore, or if it had been swallowed by the Stabilities of Portland or some other nation, or reorganized into some other political entity altogether. He had lost touch with the world in the years he'd rotted in prison, and the world hadn't waited for him. So much had changed. Was there anyplace where he belonged anymore?

That night, alone in his pup tent, the Wall smoldered

through Hanson's dreams, and for the first time in years, he felt the key move within his chest, as though the nearness to the City of God were bringing it back to life.

The next morning, they marched into the City of God, the hair rising on the back of Hanson's neck as they crossed through the palisade's gate and into the City itself. The land before them had originally looked like a vast lawn or meadow, freckled with occasional pairs of silver dots—the plates that the Utopians had used to transport themselves instantaneously from place to place—now, however, encased in crude cages of metal bars so that nobody would blunder across them to be transported who-knew-where and, more likely than not, never be seen again. The land gracefully swelled and ebbed, a park essentially, with the occasional copse of flametrees. It should have been beautiful—it *had* been beautiful once. But it was scarred with pits and trenches hacked into the land and there were black smears where stands of trees had been chopped down and burned, for what purpose Hanson could not guess. To one side, a cluster of graceful buildings or machines or whatever-they-were intruded into the parkland and they looked wrong too, some of them streaked with soot, suggesting that the Army had tried to blast them open with explosives, others ashen and wilting, like dying plants.

Down the center of the meadow was a dirt track that

led straight from the camp then suddenly jogged to one side and, after a bit, abruptly to the other before driving straight into another grouping of maybe-buildings. Those earlier soldiers who had come to loot the City of God, it appeared, had undergone their share of unpleasant adventures.

The soldiers were mostly quiet as they walked, even Delgardo seeming a bit overawed by the alien strangeness all around them, although there was some nervous speculation among the men about whether the old Utopians were somewhere inside the buildings—if buildings they were—staring ominously out at them, preparing to strike. Hanson knew better. There were no Utopians here, not in any form he understood or could recognize, anyway. But they had left thousands of their toys behind, still working, and most of them could be deadly if you blundered into them. One of the youngest soldiers, a pock-faced boy named Lopez, one cheek heavily scarred by a radiation burn, was the only one who seemed to be enjoying himself, enthusing about how beautiful and wonderful and strange everything was, until at last Sergeant Barker glumly told him, "Shut up, Lopez. You're not on fucking vacation." And Hanson surprised himself by adding, "Ai, it's pretty, but anything here can kill you in a second, without any Goddamned warning. Don't touch *anything*. Don't go through anything. Don't go under anything. And keep on the God-damned path."

Delgardo glanced back at him, and then gestured for Hanson to take the lead, although Hanson could see it hurt his pride to surrender it. "Silly to bring the only one who's been here before and then not use him as a guide, eh?" he said, and you could almost hear the unspoken words he shared with the rest of the men: *Let him be the first one to die, if something goes wrong.*

Hanson walked at the front of the group thereafter. They traveled nearly five miles that day, cautiously but steadily, along ways that had been mapped out as safe by previous incursions into the City. Bringing up the rear of their party was the Stumper, a tremendous pair of metal elephant legs which had been fitted with a wooden wagon, wheels and axles excised, atop what would have been its waist had there been more of it. It looked like a walking basket piled high with food rations, barrels of water, and other supplies and was led by a soldier tugging it along at the end of a rope.

Hanson had laughed involuntarily when he first saw the thing, and of course Delgardo demanded to know why. "Well, just look at it," Hanson said. The Stumper was made of hundreds of sliding parts that eased in and out of each other so that in motion its gleaming surface seemed to flow like water. The basket-wagon atop it was crudely designed and clumsily built. "Whatever that thing is for, it for sure a'n't just for humping cargo about. But this is the best your sort can do with it. You're like a manshogger that's found a rifle and all he can think to do with it is use it as a club."

To his surprise, Delgardo laughed, and though there were sneering overtones to it, on the whole the laughter sounded genuine. "You're one hundred percent right, Hanson, we're dealing with technology that's unfathomably beyond our comprehension, and our very best uses of it are nothing but jury-rigged kludges. Yet, for all that, a manshogger with a club has a distinct advantage over a manshogger without one."

As dusk began to fall, they made camp at the edge of an open area where multicolored tentacles of light rose from a tangle of gently swaying mists, closed ends to form shimmering rings, dwindled as they ascended, and finally disappeared with soft, musical chimes. The spectacle was probably just for looks; nevertheless, Hanson was glad that there was a stream between them and it. The soldiers got to work pitching tents and digging a slit latrine. While they did, Hanson, who had been assigned no duties, stood apart from the rest, looking at the rising loops of prismatic mists. The buildings had closed around them and then opened up again into what he thought of as a park, though God only knew what function it might actually have served. The "park" was probably safe; he'd passed through its like many a time before and never been hurt by one. But there were structures in every direction that hurt his brain if he tried to make sense of their shapes: a twisted disk taller than the Courthouse in Orange, with a square hole punched through the left half of it; a braided noodle of bright red and yellow tubes that unraveled at the top and flopped downward without quite reaching the ground; an inverted pyramid made up of rotating rectangles that Hanson almost couldn't pry his eyes away from. On the horizon, one structure soared high above the others, a series of intersecting arches with steep spires, like the sharp wings of bats hanging from a cave ceiling only reversed, which seemed to challenge the sky itself. It glowed the same eerie red-pink-gold as did the Wall itself, and that frightened him very much indeed.

The longer he stared at the thing, the more convinced he became that it—or something within it, but most likely the building itself—was staring back at him, studying him, analyzing him. Making plans.

It was making plans for Hanson specifically because he had the key within him. Delgardo believed in little healing machines because little healing machines were something a man could believe in and almost understand. But

Hanson knew better. The truth was not only stranger than a man *might* believe, it was stranger than a man *could* believe. Somehow the key was protecting him and, for whatever unfathomable reasons, Delgardo as well.

Periodically, Hanson would remember with a sudden rush of dread and loathing that was almost a seizure, the moment the key had seized him, a metal rod bursting out of Boone's dead chest, unfolding several joints, and then plunging into Hanson's chest, passing through skin and muscle and cloth as if they didn't exist, sinking out of sight within his body and leaving no trace of its existence behind.

Since then, it had always been with him, although sometimes when it was quiet inside him months and months would go by without him thinking of it at all. It was the key that had enabled him to pass alive through the Wall of the City of God, it was the key that had enabled him to seize control of the City for a critical moment, it was the key that had enabled him to shut down a section of the Wall, thus giving birth to the present they lived in now, it was the key that provided his limited "immortality," that had cured his Crab, that kept him seemingly the same age no matter how much time had gone by, maybe by creating and replenishing the little machines in his blood that Delgardo believed in but more likely by some other process, one he would never be smart enough to understand.

Throughout all the interrogations he'd endured at the prison, through all the torture and pain and mutilation and horror and humiliation, the one thing he'd never mentioned about his trip inside the City of God was the key. Sometimes it seemed as if the key itself was somehow keeping him from saying anything about it, since when they were ripping his fingernails out with red-hot tongs, and he was trying to come up with anything he could say to make them *stop,* and he tried to tell them about the key to see if that would please them, the words disappeared from his throat somehow, and he found himself unable to speak them no matter how cruelly his interrogators abused his flesh.

Thank all the gods that might exist that he *hadn't* told them, he thought now. If he had, then Overton would have written it down in his notes, and Delgardo would know about it. And if Delgardo knew . . . He was an intelligent man. It wouldn't take him long to figure out that it was the key inside Hanson's body that was replenishing his health, that was the real origin of Hanson's "immortality." And he wouldn't hesitate for a moment to rip it out of Hanson's body and claim it for his own.

And suppose that Delgardo *did* claim the key? Suppose that made it possible somehow for him to somehow seize control of the City?

That mustn't happen.

There was no way that Delgardo would relinquish the godlike power that Hanson had once refused. No, he would use it instead. Use it for his own ends, to achieve his every selfish desire and grandiose wish. He'd extend his power to affect the world outside the Wall, as Hanson had declined to do, shape it however he wanted, bend it to his will. His use of the power would grow more and more extravagant, until, with his ego, he'd try to make people worship him as a god. Which in a way, he would be—a vain, petty, cruel, ruthless god.

Most of his life, Hanson had passively drifted with the tide, doing what he was supposed to do, asking no questions, making no trouble. Even him being back in the City again was the result of being swept along by the tide of someone else's will; Delgardo had willed it, Delgardo had made it happen. All he'd done, however reluctantly, was do what he was told. Only twice in his life had he ever initiated and taken decisive action, when he'd killed Oristano the foreman, and when he opened a section of the City of God to the world. No, not even twice, because he'd been swept along on a tide of rage and pride and despair when he'd killed Oristano, unable to stop himself, hardly aware of what he was doing until it was over; there had been no planning or foresight involved, no conscious decision. So then, only one time in his miserable life had he ever decided to do something on his own, something that was his own idea, and had the will to actually make himself do it—when he'd taken down the Wall. That hadn't turned out exactly as he'd hoped that it would. But at least he'd tried. At least he'd taken action.

He couldn't afford to be passively swept along any longer. He had to *do* something, not only to get out of this situation and save his own life, but to keep Delgardo from making the world an even more horrible place than it already was.

He had to do *something.*

But what?

The soaring golden structure continued to leer down at him, silently, mockingly. At last, with a shiver, Hanson turned his back on the thing and trudged into the center of the camp, to reserve himself a place on the ground before the newly built fire and wait for food to be cooked and served.

~

That night, Hanson dreamed of his wife, Becky, carried away in the White Winter all those unhappy years ago. She was young and beautiful, with the dewy blush of youth on her skin, the way she had looked when he first met her and seen in her everything he'd ever wanted or dreamed of. After she died, he'd locked away all memories of her in the deepest recesses of his mind, but they leaked out from time to time still. Looking at her, he began to weep for all they had once had and all he had lost forever. "Hanson," she said. "This can't go on. You've got to fight back."

"I know, Becky, I know, but . . . I can't. I just can't."

"You'll be judged in the Cathedral. If you love me, you'll—"

But abruptly, he found himself in the military cemetery, searching among the graves for the body of his dead wife, unwrapping the canvas from corpse after corpse and searching the faces for her features. One canvas wrapping moved slightly as he approached and, suddenly filled with the certainty that she was after all still alive, he ripped open the cloth. Rats swarmed out, black and diseased, and when he flinched away in disgust, the corpse beneath them opened its eyes and was his old friend Boone, whose lipless mouth grinned madly and said, "Now it's your turn to die. Ha! See how *you* like it!"

~

Nobody talked about it in morning, but from the sour expressions on their faces, Hanson was sure that he wasn't the only one who'd suffered nightmares. After a cold breakfast, they broke camp and resumed their cautious march into the City. They hadn't gone more than a mile when Hanson realized that Sergeant Barker had matched strides with him and they were walking abreast. Quietly, without looking his way, Barker said, "Stop baiting Delgardo."

"Eh?" Hanson did not look at Barker either but continued walking along, scanning the City ahead, looking for trouble.

"Standing up to his kind don't get y'nothing but trouble. He's the commander. He's got the law on his side, he's got guns on his side, he's got *me* on his side. You got nothing, an' a man with nothing had best keep his head down. Hear what I'm saying?"

"Ai."

"'Nuff said, then." Barker slowed his pace, drifting back along the line. It touched Hanson that the sergeant would be looking out after him like that, though he doubted it was done out of any altruistic impulse. Men like Barker believed in keeping things calm, in damping things down before trouble had a chance to flare up. Hanson doubted very much that Barker could prevent the trouble that was brewing between him and Delgardo. But he admired him for trying.

Not long after, the stream curved to block their way. Luckily, there was a lacquered red bridge: wooden, arched, with railings to either side, looking perfectly out of place in its ordinariness. After a brief consultation with Delgardo, Hanson went over it by himself, each plank making a musical sound as he trod on it. When he reached the far side safely, he waved and the others ran across in a storm of bridge-song.

They were now beyond the previous explored areas, so there was no path to follow. Hanson asked Delgardo what they were looking for, and how he was supposed to find it when he didn't know where they were going, but Delgardo had just looked scornful and said, "I'll know it when I see it!," although Hanson got the feeling that the smug air of superiority was only a facade to cover his own uncertainty. As Hanson had feared they would, they were heading toward the golden building-thing that had filled him with unease the night before. *The Cathedral,* he thought, and wondered where he had heard that name before. But at least it still seemed a good way off.

They had stopped for a break when they were startled by a sudden cry of fear. One of the soldiers—Miller? Fiske? Hanson was still having difficulty remembering who was who—had wandered a bit ahead and was pointing at a stand of flowering dwarf sequoias. A dark silhouette no thicker than his hand and as large as an elephant was picking its way daintily out of the trees. It had five long legs, all of different sizes, that tapered to points at the bottom and joined to form a hunched, headless torso at the top. The soldier raised his rifle to shoot at it.

Running with a speed he was amazed he was still capable of, Hanson managed to reach the soldier before he could fire and roughly seized the rifle barrel, pushing it to the side. "You don't need to do that. It's harmless. It's a . . . a . . . a gardener. It plants seeds and trims trees, that's all." As they watched, the gardener paused to scoop a hole in the turf and then, with another limb, plucked a seedling from within its shadowy interior, and gently settled it into place. "A'n't nothing to be afraid of." Except, Hanson thought, for some other device, lurking unseen, that might take action to protect the gardener, if they looked like they might damage it. He'd run afoul of one such, before, and didn't look forward to a second bout.

"I'm not afraid of nothing!" the boy snapped. He snatched away his rifle and indignantly started back toward the others. His path, though, was different from the meandering way he had come for, with shocking abruptness, something seized him and slammed him to the ground. Struggling weakly, pressed flat to the ground, obviously unable to rise, he cried, "Help! Help! It's crushing me!"

The soldiers came running. At a barked order from Delgardo, two of them flung themselves down on the ground and crawled rapidly forward on their elbows to seize Dawkins—Hanson had decided it was neither Miller or Fiske, but rather Dawkins—by the ankles. Four more soldiers seized the legs of those two and pulled, so that, almost effortlessly, Dawkins was slid backward and out of the crushing zone, where gravity was, apparently, many times greater than it was in the ordinary world.

Sergeant Barker unbuttoned Dawkins's shirt and examined his torso with a gentleness that could not have been bettered by the boy's own mother before pronouncing him shaken but fundamentally unhurt. "There'll be bruising," he said, "that's all."

Hanson put a hand on the young man's shoulder. "You're lucky," he said. "That's good. Lucky is a good thing to be." He paused, thought better of what he was about to say, and then thought better of not saying it. "Don't push that luck too far, though, a'right?" Turning away, he shouted, "Somebody fetch me a sack of flour!"

When one of the soldiers—Chan? Phillips? Marini?—had passed the flour to Hanson from the supplies on the Stumper, he dug a hand deep inside it and then flung the hand outward. White dust floated in the air. He took three steps forward and flung another handful. It too floated away. Two steps forward, a third fist of flour. This time, however, the flour drifted on the air—and then suddenly slammed to the ground.

Hanson grunted in satisfaction. The other times he

had tried this trick, he'd had to use sand. Flour was much better. He flung further handfuls to either side of the stain. They too slammed downward.

Systematically, with meticulous caution, Hanson walked up and down the sharp-edged line of white, until it was clear that it was wider in one direction than the other. He continued to fling flour and follow the narrow white triangle he was creating until its two sides fined down to a point, touching a small, glowing purple tile set in the ground. It could have been covered by a thumb. "A'right. It's marked now. Just go 'round by the front and you'll be fine."

Delgardo, smiling, turned to Hanson. "Is this something you saw before?"

"Ai."

"Did it never occur to you to dig there, when you found one of these spots?"

"No," Hanson answered, not seeing the point, "it never did. Sir."

"Manshogger!" Delgardo said, almost fondly. Then, turning back to his men, he commanded, "Shovels out! Dig here!"

Several minutes' painstaking work unearthed . . . *something*. It was deep red, the size of a man's forearm, slick-surfaced, and smelled of cinnamon. Delgardo passed a hand over its surface and it turned emerald green. "It's off now," he said, and tossed it to one of his men. "Wrap that up and stow it away in the Stumper." Then, raising his voice, "We made our first find, boys!"

They cheered.

To his horror, Hanson heard himself ask, "What is it?"

"No idea," Delgardo said cheerily, giving him a hearty whack between the shoulder blades. "Down at the front, they've figured out how to put it to good use and they call it a gravity gun. But I seriously doubt it was ever intended to be used as a weapon, don't you?"

Hanson shrugged.

"We manshoggers, though . . . We can turn almost anything into a weapon. That's our gift. It's what separates you and me from the animals." Without transition, Delgardo pointed toward the distant golden building. "We've been walking for hours and the Cathedral hasn't gotten any closer. How far away do you think it is? How big do you think it is?"

"I've got a bad feeling about that thing. I don't think we should go there," Hanson said, remembering only at the last instant to add, "sir." He did not mention the sensation, which he could not shake, that it was *studying* him, nor his suspicion that it was keeping its distance, moving on enormous legs, perhaps, the way some of the structures in the City could, while it made up its mind what to do about them. Nor did he ask how Delgardo knew its name.

Delgardo laughed. "You want to live forever, Hanson?" he said sarcastically. Then he shouted to the soldiers, "Get your asses in gear, boys! I bet we can reach that sumbitch by sundown."

Not long after that conversation, they lost their first soldier.

8

THEIR PROGRESS WAS SLOW, for they had to constantly scan the land before them for potential dangers and, though Phillips (if that's who it is) carefully charted their way on gridded mapping paper, their compasses did not work here at all, so they had to rely on dead reckoning, with the Cathedral as their one fixed landmark.

Shortly after their midday break for lunch, the buildings drew away and they found themselves facing a grid of enormous stones, twice the height of a man, set up like menhirs, all dissimilar, with between them gravel and nothing more. They stretched as far as the eye could see to either side and looked to extend as far ahead. At the sight of them, Hanson immediately turned and began walking east.

"Hold it right there," Delgardo snapped. "Where do you think you're going?"

"I told you. Never go through anything, under anything, inside anything, or between anything. If you want to survive. Sir."

Delgardo looked scornful. "Have you ever heard of

gongshi, Hanson? No, of course you haven't. Chinese scholar's stones. Rocks that were selected for their aesthetic value and used as objects of meditation. Look at these things, what do you see? No two of them are alike. Different kinds, different shapes. What we've got here is somebody's rock collection. Probably the owner liked to wander through it, thinking profound thoughts. None of us are afraid of a rock garden, am I right?" Lowering his voice so he couldn't be overheard, Delgardo added, "And I'll put three rounds through your skull if you don't lead us straight across. Maybe you'd survive that. But I don't think you'd enjoy the experience much."

So, having no choice, Hanson led the troop into the rocks.

It was eerily quiet among the great stones. Not a bird or insect was anywhere to be seen or heard. The only sound was the crunch of gravel underfoot. Nobody spoke a word. Somehow, this near-silence translated, in the inner reaches of his brain, into a sensation of profoundest peace. After a few minutes, Hanson found his thoughts wandering back to his youth, to the days when his wife, Becky, was still alive and he was in possession of his full force of strength and vigor. Those were good times, though they had seemed hard enough then. He'd put in his ten hours at the factory, shoveling coal, and sometimes have a watery beer with friends in somebody's basement speakeasy before returning home to his wife and dinner. There was never enough money to keep lots of lights burning, so in his memories, Becky's face had a warm orange glow, all the rest of the world falling away from her into darkness. For the first few years, they two were so very, very happy.

He didn't like to think about what came after.

Better to cast his thoughts further back, to his childhood, when he had been the protector of his little sister from schoolyard bullies. He'd always been larger than the other kids in his class, so at recess the little bastards would sometimes deftly arrange, by lies and rumors, for him to fight an upperclassman. Sometimes he'd win and sometimes not. But the image of him as a bruiser, with blood on his knuckles and a glower on his face, lingered and he rarely had to do more than growl a word or two of warning to keep the bullies away from her. She'd died young, his sister had, but while she lived, she adored him, had little—

Little—

Why couldn't he remember her name?

Hanson stumbled and drew himself to a stop. Head swimming, he put out a hand to keep from falling, and felt himself lurch against one of the standing stones. Delgardo, who had been following in his wake, brushed past as if he weren't there. The others, too, he saw, were plodding along steadily, eyes half closed, heads bowed, like so many sleepwalkers. They passed him by without a glance, and he had to dance backward to avoid being stepped on by the Stumper, which, had it been a foot or two wider would have been scraping against the rocks to either side of it.

"Everybody! Everybody!" Hanson shouted. "Wake up!" He grabbed hold of the kid who was leading the Stumper by a rope and shook his shoulders. The soldier snorted and his eyes fluttered open. Then he ran forward to shake—Phillips, was it?—and then Barker, and then he and Barker were running up and down the line, shouting and shaking, until everyone was awake again.

With puzzled expressions, the men listened to Hanson as he tried to explain: that the rocks were somehow mesmerizing them all, putting them into a half-sleep for whatever purpose he couldn't say, it was possible the rocks were making them forget things, maybe they ate memories, he couldn't say, but . . . "Listen to me!" Sergeant Barker said. "The first one of you falls asleep, I will kick your ass halfway to the moon. Understand?"

"Sir! Yes, sir!" the men said, as one.

"A'right. Now. Double time! March!"

They were moving again, fast this time. The sergeant danced up and down the line, shouting and punching, keeping everyone going. And it worked. In less than an hour they were out of the rock garden.

When Delgardo had called a halt, Hanson drew him aside. "Listen. Sir. There's something you need to know."

"I was trying to remember . . ." Delgardo said in such an unguarded, puzzled way as to seem, for the briefest and most fleeting of moments, almost human. "A girl I knew. She . . ." He shook his head. Then, registering how Hanson was looking at him, "What is it?"

"There were a dozen of us when we started out, right?"

Delgardo squinted at him, as if he were something unexpected and not particularly pleasant. "Yeah. So?"

"I only count eleven now. But . . . I can't quite remember who we've lost."

Delgardo was still for a long moment, clearly running over the roster in his mind and failing to come up with a name. At last he said, "Well, whoever he is, he's not coming back. Don't say anything about this to the men. That's an order, Hanson."

"Yes, sir." Hanson didn't like being polite to the bastard. But Delgardo looked like he would make Hanson sorry if he wasn't.

"Fifteen minutes!" Delgardo said at the top of his voice. "Then we get going again."

~

They were following an open space between enormous cylinders that Hanson did his best not to look at, because they were covered with what appeared to be beetles the size of his hand and in constant motion, when Hanson saw that ahead of them was a narrow silver arch. It was three times as tall as a man and, because it touched the cylinders to either side, impossible to walk around. Reflexively, without even thinking, Hanson turned away.

"Halt!" Delgardo commanded. Then, "Why are you going out of your way here? You know something about this hoop?"

"Never go through anything," Hanson mumbled. "Never go underneath anything. Never put your hand inside anything. It might be safe, it might not. Best way is to never find out."

"But you don't know anything specific about this thing? You haven't seen its like before?"

"No," Hanson said, "sir."

Delgardo pulled up a handful of grass, bringing up a clod of dirt with it. He threw the thing through the hoop and it fell to the ground with a soft plop. Then he unsnapped his holster and with meaningful intensity, said, "Looks fine to me. Walk on through."

Everybody stood motionless, staring at Hanson. They were none of them his friends and they all carried weapons with a confidence that said they knew how to use them. He swiftly added up all his options and, as usual, came up with zero. Then he took a deep breath and obeyed.

He walked through the hoop.

Nothing happened.

"You see?" Delgardo said and, jauntily stepping through the hoop himself, waved for the soldiers to follow him.

Hanson was looking forward and so did not see what happened next, for which he would be forever grateful. However, what he heard as the first of the soldiers passed through the hoop was a strangely liquid sound which made him spin around in his tracks. Just in time to see a tangle of what looked to be internal organs slump to the ground. Blood poured freely from it.

On the far side of the hoop, one of the soldiers bent over and threw up. "He's been turned *inside-out,*" another whispered in horrified awe. "Oh shit, Lopez," Sergeant Barker said, making the sign to ward off the Evil Eye. "Poor kid!"

What had been Lopez lay all in a heap, his innards glistening in the sun. Intermingled with them were bones, strangely twisted into shapes that Hanson's mind could not quite manage to make sensible. At the center of it all was what had to be a core of muscles and skin and cloth. It smelled like the foulest sewer in creation.

The whole wet mass twisted and flopped, suggesting that the soldier was still alive and attempting to bring his body under control again. And it made a noise—a high, weak shrill like violin strings being stroked by someone with no idea how to play them. Which could only be, Hanson realized with horror, the man trying to scream.

"You," Delgardo said, pointing to the nearest soldier. "Front and center."

The soldier snapped to and stood at attention. His face was stone. You had to look at his eyes, which were showing the whites, to see how scared he was.

The screaming continued, a high, unbearable noise.

"Right there—" Delgardo pointed down at a bright pink mass that was surely the brain. "Stomp down on it hard."

"Sir!" the soldier said, but he didn't move, just stood swaying and sweating and looking as if he was about to throw up.

"Oh, for the love of—" Delgardo pushed the soldier roughly aside. He stepped forward, raised his foot, and stomped.

There was a squelching noise and everybody looked away.

But the screaming stopped.

Delgardo glared at Hanson as if *he'd* been the one to ignore a direct order, then snapped, "Burial detail! You,

you, and you. Be careful you don't step through the hoop."

~

When the body had been properly buried—nobody commented on the color or the texture or the smell of the soil it was interred in—Delgardo, who hadn't looked at Hanson once in the time it took to dig the grave, said to the man who'd been leading the Stumper, "Stretch out your hands as far apart as you can, and then cut me a length of rope exactly that long." Then, to Hanson, "Take off your shirt."

"It wasn't *me* that—"

"You had one job," Delgardo said with icy calm. "To keep us safe. Yet you let Lopez walk through that hoop. For that, you get ten lashes. I'd like to make it a hell of a lot more, but we still need you ambulatory. Consider yourself lucky. Now, take your shirt off, you damned ape!" he roared, his voice rising for the first time. He made a good pretense of outrage, but as Hanson unbuttoned his shirt, he knew what was really going on here. Delgardo had just gotten one of his own men killed; if he was to continue leading them at all effectively—and one of them had already been at the point of mutiny—he needed to slough off the blame on somebody else: a scapegoat. Hanson. It wasn't fair, but it did make a kind of sense, and that made the punishment that followed just a little easier to bear. Not much, but some. At least *something* made sense in this mad city. At least something could be understood.

It was working, too. Hanson could tell that by the way the soldiers' jaws tightened and their eyes glistened as they watched each lash fall. It was clear to see how much they were enjoying this. Somebody even laughed when he cried out in pain. They hated him and they savored every blow. Delgardo was one of them, but Hanson was the stranger, the outsider, and it was *his* fault they were here, in this awful place. If they hadn't been here, if they hadn't had to bring Hanson here, Lopez would still be alive.

Alone among them all, only Sergeant Barker stared down at the ground during the punishment. It struck Hanson that he had a disappointed look on his face, as if his problem child—Hanson—had, somehow, let him down. After one long glance, Hanson determined to look anywhere but at him. Somehow, his quiet disapproval made the ordeal worse.

At last, his punishment was over. Hanson got painfully to his feet and clumsily began to button his shirt. Delgardo turned away, avoiding eye contact. Perhaps he felt some guilt over Lopez's death, perhaps even some embarrassment for sloughing off the responsibility onto Hanson, for he certainly must know whose fault it *really* was that Lopez had been killed, and know also that Hanson knew that he knew, no matter how much rage he pretended to feel to cover it up.

~

On the third day, they were walking through vast lawns with scattered clumps of fruiting elms and the occasional building-or-artifact which Delgardo made no attempt to examine, when the trees abruptly gave way to what appeared to be a forest of termite mounds. Some were small and others as large as buildings and there were thousands upon thousands of them. The Cathedral loomed up on the far side, drawing Delgardo onward like his own personal North Star or maybe that white whale that old wives told little children about, perpetually hunted by a mad sea-captain yet somehow always escaping at the last minute. Hanson remembered those stories fondly, remembered how he'd always rooted for the whale, though even then he'd suspected that in the real world it would long ago have been killed, flensed, and its blubber rendered down into lamp oil.

Delgardo, though, was not looking at the Cathedral but at the termite mounds. Rubbing his chin, he said,

"Let's go take a look, just you and me." After telling his men to take a break—they could use it too; to a man, they looked ashen for weariness and want of sleep—he led Hanson to the nearest mound. Up close, they could see that the surfaces of the things were riddled with tunnels and that little metal insects came and went from them.

Delgardo picked up an insect and examined it closely. "It's a machine of some kind. And it's carrying a speck of metal. Copper, I think." He set the insect-machine on the mound and it disappeared into one of the tunnels. Then he laid a hand on the mound. "The surface is crumbly, like dried clay," he said to nobody in particular. Pressing his ear to it, he said, "There's a grinding noise, like thousands of tiny gears. Some parts of the surface are warmer than others. Over there, I see one with a slick of ice on its north side. Wait here."

At an imperious wave from Delgardo, the soldier in charge of the Stumper made it kneel. Delgardo rummaged within, came up with a shovel, and returned, whistling, with it slung over his shoulder. "Watch and learn," he said, and swung the shovel with all his might. The dried surface exploded into powder, and metal insects rained down from the mound, clattering to the ground.

Five strong blows and the top of the mound was gone,

revealing what looked to be a half-melted machine in its interior. It was as bright as quicksilver and had what looked to be many-fingered arms, at least a dozen of them. "There!" Delgardo said proudly. He shoved the shovel in the ground, adding, "Do you see it now?"

Hanson stared at the thing, trying to see whatever it was that Delgardo saw. At last, baffled, he shook his head mutely.

"It's a factory, you lout. The City needs machines to do its maintenance, and those machines are built—or assembled, or maybe even grown—right here. This is the mother lode. All we need do is post soldiers here and every time one of these factories hatches, snatch whatever comes out. This is everything I promised my superiors I'd find, and more. Enough for a promotion, a raise in pay, and a good start on a political career at an absolute minimum."

"So we're going back now?" Hanson asked, not really believing for an instant they were.

"Are you mad? Of course not. There's so much more to be found! These are just things. What I'm after is power." Something in Hanson's expression amused Delgardo greatly, then, for he said, "Oh, no, no, no, not the crude sort of power that has to be employed on the likes of you because it's the only thing that you understand. Not the power to hurt and to kill and to create misery. Every human being in existence has that power. I'm talking about the power to shape history, to bring about real, significant change, to remake the world in my own image. That's what I'm after."

What you're after is death, Hanson thought. But he didn't say it out loud.

~

By twisty, laborious ways, the patrol passed through the factories and finally came to the last of the mounds. The land beyond was fair and open and carpeted with low, blood red grasses. The usual variety of enigmatic structures, all potentially lethal, rose up here and there. But the golden Cathedral was nowhere to be seen.

Delgardo cursed and spat when he realized that, and, spinning, seized Hanson by the arm. "You've led us astray, you coward! You traitor! Deliberately too, I'll bet anything you did."

With an angry jerk of his thumb skyward, Hanson said, "Look up there. That's the sun. Which means *that* way is east and *that* way west, so we're facing due north. Factories to our back. We're standing where the Cathedral was. Only it a'n't here anymore. It's as simple as that."

"Buildings don't just get up and walk away."

"Here they do. Face it, Delgardo—the Cathedral just

doesn't want to talk with you." Watching Delgardo's face, Hanson thought fleetingly that the moment had come at last, the one he had been dreading all along, when they two would have to fight, most likely to the death. Truth be told, he suspected he might win. But in the aftermath, there would be the soldiers to deal with, and he knew for certain that would not go well for him. But he saw Delgardo, with an effort, rein in his anger, reasserting control over himself, and saw, too, behind his animal rage traces of uncertainty and, yes, even fear. Delgardo had no idea how to make the Cathedral come to him or, for that matter, how to keep himself alive while he tried. Out of nowhere, Hanson experienced a strange elation. *We may be in Hell,* he thought, *but I know the rules here better than you do.*

~

That evening, Hanson couldn't help noting how listlessly the soldiers pitched tents, cooked food, ate, took up guard duty. They were all suffering from lack of sleep and none of them looked forward to the nightmares that would accompany what little sleep they might manage. By contrast, he and Delgardo were doing fine—courtesy of the key, he imagined. But as for the others . . . Nights filled with bad dreams and days with structures that hurt the eye to look upon and the mind to contemplate, accompanied by the constant possibility of sudden death, had taken their toll, breaking down the soldiers. Before too long they'd start getting careless, wander into buildings and get eaten by strange machines, lie down on the sleek ceramic plates that Sergeant Barker had warned that, on an earlier incursion, he had witnessed turn men into animals like nothing anybody had ever seen. Not long after that, the survivors would begin to suspect the worst of one another before remembering at last that they had weapons and the training to use them. He sat up, thinking, for a time and then went to Delgardo's tent, which was, of course, twice the size of anyone else's. He rattled the flap and said, "Get your clothes on. We need to talk."

Delgardo dressed and followed Hanson away from the tents. They walked around a dome whose surface glowed with images of what might be rocks or, equally plausibly, platelets of blood, floating silently, occasionally bumping into one another, and noiselessly bouncing apart, shedding flowers like sparks. There, out of sight of the camp, they stopped.

"So?" Delgardo said.

"I've been watching the men. You must see it too. A few more days of this is going to kill them."

Delgardo grinned a shark's grin that seemed to have

too many teeth in it for anything human. "Why, Hanson," he said, "that's what they're here for, isn't it? To die a little, if called upon. What the hell do you think a soldier *is* if not somebody who's paid to die for you?"

"Send them back." The soldiers had the maps they had made on the way in. The sun would orient them. The thought of getting out of this madness would give them focus, keep them wary. Hanson was sure they could make it out alive, most of them, anyway, and possibly all.

"They're not your pals, Hanson. I'm sure you've noticed that fact. They don't even like you—and, yes, I acknowledge that's primarily my doing." Delgardo spread his arms and made a theatrical little bow. "So why should you, much less I, care about their well-being?"

"They're . . . they're people, after all," Hanson mumbled. By the light of the dome, he could see how much Delgardo was enjoying this verbal sparring match. Of course, he'd never been much of a talker, or very good at logic, but the imbalance of competence clearly didn't bother Delgardo one bit. A duel in which the opponent was unarmed and he held a battle ax would only make the whole affair that much sweeter to him.

"Why, so is everybody. So are the Southerners and we mowed them down without mercy not a week ago. They didn't ask for special treatment, did they? No, and didn't get any. So why should I—" Delgardo stopped, frozen in mid-speech by a sudden realization. "You know something! You big, stupid bastard, you know something about the Cathedral, and you've been keeping it from me."

"Ai."

With a wordless cry of rage, Delgardo ran at Hanson, fists balled. Hanson had never been a particularly skilled fighter, but he was strong as an ox, and he knew how to punch. His huge fist crashed into Delgardo's face. A flare of pain in Hanson's hand, the sound of breaking bone, a spurt of blood, and Delgardo went down as if he'd been shot, sprawled flat on his back.

Hanson waited.

For a long time Delgardo did not move. Time enough for Hanson to slip away and disappear into the jungle of strangeness that he knew a hundred times better than Delgardo ever would. Instead, he stood motionless, listening to the man's ragged breathing. At last, Delgardo moaned, rolled over on his side, and sat up. Drawing a silk handkerchief from his pocket, he used it to stanch the flow of blood from his nose. He glared at Hanson with hatred that burned like a flame, but there was a touch of respect intermingled therein as well, something that Hanson had never seen before in him.

"The Cathedral has been thinking about what to do with us and it's just about made up its mind. Right now it's waiting for me to accept that I have no choice but to talk to it." Hanson could not have said how he knew all this, but he did. "You want to get into the Cathedral? I can make it happen. Only, you have to send your men home first. That's my price."

Slowly Delgardo got to his feet, handkerchief to nose. "You do realize," he said casually, "that when all this is over, I'm going to make you pay, and pay dearly, for hitting me."

Hanson gaped at him in astonishment. "You honestly think that we're both going to get out of this alive?" Something rose up within him, an unfamiliar tickling, and, while Delgardo stared at him in disbelief, he found himself first chortling and then roaring with laughter.

He laughed until he cried. Long before he was done, Delgardo had stomped away, back to his tent.

That night, for the first time since entering the City of God, Hanson slept well.

~

In the morning, Hanson awoke to discover that the Cathedral was looming over the camp, its walls not a hundred paces distant, and dazzling to look upon. Up close it was as large as a mountain—no, larger! The soldiers appeared dazed and confused, save for the two night guards, whom Sergeant Barker was bawling out while they frantically tried to explain that they'd been alert all night and nothing had happened, nothing had moved, the Cathedral was just *there* when the sun came up.

Delgardo, meanwhile, had his head tilted back and was gawking up at the spires that glittered and gleamed in the morning sunshine. He turned away from the Cathedral, saw Hanson, and they exchanged a glance. *Believe me now?* Hanson thought, knowing that his onetime torturer and now open enemy would be able to read it on his face. Delgardo gave him a short, sharp nod, and then turned to the sergeant. "Lay off those men! This has nothing to do with them. Send somebody to my tent to fetch the folding chair and my portable writing desk."

Then, sitting with the writing desk on his lap, Delgardo delicately filled his pen from a bottle of ink and wrote out a letter, which he read aloud at the end of each sentence loudly enough for all to hear, explaining that the troop was returning to base without him by his express command, and concluding: *We have made great discoveries and I confidently expect to make many more.* He signed the document with a flourish, blew on the ink to help it dry, then folded it and sealed it with wax and his signet ring.

Delgardo handed the letter to Sergeant Barker, saying,

"You have your orders. Break camp and make for base. Be sure to bring along all my effects. If this goes as I believe it will, they'll be sacred relics one day and kept in a museum for all to admire."

"Sir. Yes, sir." The relief on Sergeant Barker's face was almost painful to look upon.

Soon thereafter, Hanson and Delgardo were alone. "I've kept my end of the bargain," Delgardo said. "Now it's time you keep yours."

~

The Cathedral rose steep and sheer in front of them, pinks and roses and corals blending into one another so that its surface seemed to shimmer. As they grew closer, Hanson could feel the heat it radiated, fierce and stinging; nevertheless, he forced himself to walk steadily toward it. Delgardo walked by his side. When Hanson glanced his way, he looked confident and unafraid, two traits that Hanson himself decidedly did not share. He kept walking anyway. He did not see that there was any other choice, the Cathedral wanted him to do this and it clearly had the power to enforce its wishes. Also, if Delgardo was going to make a grab for power, Hanson wanted to be there to make certain he didn't get it.

When he came to the windowless, featureless side of

the Cathedral, there was a searing blast of heat and a flare of agony. Then he was alone, in a moving bubble that kept pace with him as he walked, just as had happened when he had walked through the Wall itself. There was an opalescent light in here, although nothing to see by it, and the air was getting hotter with every step. A buzzing sound rose up, like millions of angry bees. As he pushed forward, the buzzing grew louder and louder, filling his head, making his teeth ache. By God, it was hot! The heat, too, kept increasing, until he was sure that his skin must be burning and blackening. Pain was a constant, impossible for him to ignore. The buzzing filled the whole world now, and he stumbled and nearly fell, but he kept pushing forward. Keep going, keep going—

Then, suddenly, he was in a room filled with cool gray light.

Delgardo stepped out of the wall and looked about with interest. "What now?" he asked.

"I . . . I don't . . ."

"What is it?" Delgardo asked in an irritable voice. "What is it you don't?"

". . . feel so good."

Then Hanson screamed as the key, which had lain quiescent within him for so long, came bursting out of his chest, sending him falling backward, uncoiling itself from within his guts, unfolding in a series of jointed cylinders, then twisting together again, melding, softening, changing color, becoming something else—and all the while, causing so much pain that Hanson had just reached the conclusion that he was about to die when, without warning, everything went dark.

~

When Hanson came to, he was lying on the floor of the featureless gray room. Nearby, Delgardo sat cross-legged, chatting with a woman similarly seated. Hearing him stir, Delgardo looked over his shoulder and amiably said, "So this is the secret you've been hiding, Hanson. Any other man would have told me everything about the key back in prison. But I see now that all my efforts were in vain. I could have keep torturing you until doomsday and you still wouldn't have blabbed." He applauded lightly. "Kudos to you, Hanson. Kudos!"

But Hanson wasn't listening to Delgardo's words. Instead, he stared, transfixed, at the woman sitting across the room from him.

"Becky?" he said.

He felt dazed, poleaxed. It was his wife, his *dead* wife, only somehow, miraculously, restored to the dewy flush of youth that had been hers when they first met—before the hard years, before the shortages, the food riots, the recurrent plagues. Before the stillbirths, the formal declaration that an unsympathetic doctor had so baldly made that she would never be able to produce a living child, before the . . .

Before the hemorrhagic infection that had carried her off.

Becky smiled that warm, loving smile that Hanson had missed so achingly for so many terrible years. "Hello, Carl." She reached out and took his hand.

~

Hanson and Becky were strolling hand in hand together through the City of God. A light breeze, perfumed with cinnamon and sandalwood, ruffled her hair, and though they were surrounded by Utopian devices and dwellings, for the first time since passing through the Wall, Hanson felt not the least fear of the City, for he understood everything here, both what it did and why, from the glass clouds floating overhead to the halls of shadow and the soft burrowers underfoot. Hanson did not know how such knowledge was possible. He knew only that he was very, very happy and that it was all a Goddamned lie. To his horror, he began to cry.

Becky turned a face toward him that was all sweet, loving concern. "You mustn't reject this, Carl. It can all, myself included, be yours."

"You're not Becky," Hanson said. It was not so much a statement as a fervent plea that she somehow prove him wrong. Everything within him wanted this woman to be his wife, his one love, his Rebekah. Only his reason insisted that she wasn't.

She hugged his arm. "I am not and yet I could be." A gardener moved gracefully past them, scattering little turquoise lizards in its wake. "You've probably guessed that I'm the key. But you have no idea what that is, do you?" Hanson shook his head and she sighed. "Link arms with me. I may not be your wife, but I've lived with you more intimately than even she did, and I've learned more about you than ever she could." He did as she bade him, and she led him onward. "Do you see that menhir at the top of the hill before us?"

"The big stone, you mean?"

"Yes. Come with me there. I want you to meet my mother."

The stone, when they came to it, was gray and weathered. It stood up on end and was twice as tall as either of them. Letting go of Hanson, Becky bowed deeply before it. "Mother, awaken!" The surface of the stone shimmered and flowed. A blast of heat went out from it and it changed color, brightening into fluid reds, pinks, corals, peaches. It was the same color as the Cathedral and Hanson got the distinct impression that they were somehow connected, that between them was a vast subterranean body of which the Cathedral was an outthrust knee, perhaps, and this stone but the tip of a raised pointer finger.

Though it terrified him, Hanson stood his ground. "What is...? You say this is your *mother*?"

Out of nowhere, a voice both female and infinitely sad, spoke. "I am the City... and I am so very, very lonely."

~

At the end of their conversation, Becky—or the key, or whatever she really was—let go of Hanson's hand and he was back in the gray room inside the Cathedral. Delgardo, that insufferable ass, immediately began talking. "Do you realize, Hanson," he said, "that our ancestors were given the option of entering the City of God before its Wall was raised? While you were unconscious, I learned so much from this young lady! The idiots turned down the opportunity, some for religious reasons, others for politics, and still others because they feared the unknown. They were all damned fools. They could have had infinite wealth, and they chose misery instead. The Utopians called them the Renunciates and banned them—us—from the City forever."

Annoyed, Hanson flicked his fingers in a dismissive

gesture, one that, though he had no thought of it at the time, echoed that with which Overton used to dismiss him from their "conversations," as he called them. "They're dead and we're alive. I'd say we got the better of the deal."

"Not dead," Becky said. "Transformed."

"I don't know what she means by that, Hanson," Delgardo said, boyishly, transparently eager to move the focus of conversation back to himself, "though I asked a great many questions. The cogent point here is that they left behind a City that was built to serve people. What could it do? Welcome in more? But in very little time, the new City-dwellers would grow as decadent as the Utopians were. So it conceived the idea of an order of caretakers. People who would have control over the City's resources but only share them with the worthy. Incorruptible guardians who would ensure that the City's power was never misused. So Becky—the key—was sent out to find someone who could found that order." It was obvious from his smug demeanor who Delgardo thought that Someone should be.

"It sounds good," Hanson said, shaking his head like an ox. "I mean, it *sounds* good. But . . ." He thought of all the bosses he had known—perfectly decent men, some of them, before they'd been given the position, coworkers you'd be proud to share a drink with; others, of course, not—and what power over others had done to them. It turned them cruel, petty, erratic, vindictive. Remove the worst of bosses and replace him with the best of laborers and, within the year, their own mothers wouldn't be able distinguish the new boss from the old. "Who guards us from the guardians?"

Becky laid a loving hand on his shoulder. Her eyes glowed. "You do."

Delgardo shot to his feet, outraged. "No! Not him—not this oafish, blundering fool! He couldn't be trusted to—"

"Mother?" Becky said. "We don't need this one anymore."

Golden tentacles arose from the floor, the walls, the ceiling, wrapping themselves about Delgardo, pinning his arms, holding his legs motionless, gagging his mouth. They were not burning hot, as when Hanson had walked through the Cathedral's substance. But Delgardo was clearly helpless within their grip. His eyes were wide with fear.

Becky stood, pulling Hanson to his feet after her. "What do you want done with him? He can't be allowed to live, obviously. Do you want him to die quickly, without pain—or slowly, in great agony?"

"He's a bad man," Hanson said, "and I don't s'pose that

he deserves to live. But I've killed two men in my time and that's stain enough for a lifetime. Just . . . let him go, a'right? Out into the City to find his way home alone. That can be his punishment, I guess. Maybe he'll learn better someday."

Becky's face melted into a look of purest joy. "You choose mercy! You've passed the final test."

Then she nodded, and the tentacles contracted, soundlessly squeezing all the life from Delgardo's body.

9

ONCE A YEAR, never more, the abbot liked to go off by himself, jug in hand, to the top of a grassy hill overlooking the City of God, where he would get good and drunk and howl at the moon. The first-year friars, idealistic young recruits to a man, were always shocked. But, "Never you mind," the older friars would say. "He a'n't hurting nobody, 'specially not you. A man needs to blow off steam every now and then. 'Specially one like old Hanson. He's been through a lot, that one, but he's a good man just the same. You wait and see. You'll learn."

There was a full moon tonight and the summer breeze was sultry and soft. Hanson let the jug drop with a soft thud and then guided his aged butt down alongside it. He kicked off his sandals so he could dig his toes into the cool grass. He didn't really see the point of the sandals and the robes and cincture and the bells and the prayers, to tell the truth of it. So far as he could see, it was all just playacting. But it helped to keep the men honest, he supposed. Hanson had had it all explained to him by respectful subordinates so often that he had to wonder, sometimes, why they didn't just get rid of such a thick-headed, useless old ox as himself in favor of someone smarter.

Still, he was a legend, he supposed, and that counted for a lot. He was the one who had uprooted two-thirds of the City of God and sent it striding out into the world. It was Hanson who had initiated the Age of Miracles in which Utopian devices dug and burrowed and scrubbed and cleaned—undoing the radioactive hot spots from forgotten wars, cleansing the springs and streams and rivers that no one had dared drink from for centuries, healing the soil that now produced astonishing yields of crops the equal of anything from Utopian times. They were still out there somewhere, he supposed, digging and burrowing and scrubbing and cleaning. The world was a large place. It would take a long time for even the most efficient machines to stalk their way around it.

Hanson uncorked the jug and took a swig.

Ahhh. Improve the world all you like, one thing never changed: hooch was hooch and thank God for that. Hanson could feel the tension in his shoulders begin to ease. The friars he was responsible for were decent fellows, on the whole, just as the sisters who answered to Becky—Reverend Mother Rebekah, as she was now called—were, by repute, good women. By mutual agreement he and Becky kept their flocks isolated from one another; hers to one end of the city, his to the other. Still, you couldn't keep them entirely apart, not when the stepping-plates meant that no two places in the City of God were more than a few hundred paces apart. So there would of necessity be gossip, incidents, unexplained pregnancies, but nothing more than you would expect from honest, backsliding, self-deluding human beings. There was weakness in the best of them. But, so far as he could see, no real malice.

Still, they could be a bothersome lot. Like the two that the Reverend Mother's people had caught and then written him about, asking for his judgment. As if he had the slightest notion what to do with them! Or self-righteous, like Friar Lorenz, who had come into his office this morning with an indignant expression and a sheath of yellow flimsies that turned out to be requests for seven vortex engines from the Stabilities of Portland. "The insolence of them!" the friar had snapped. "Their messenger made it clear that these are demands, not requests. Demands!"

Hanson studied the papers, pretending to understand them much better than he actually did. "These are for the new seaport they're building?"

"Yes."

With a sigh, Hanson handed them back. "Tell the messenger that we only have five available at the moment. He can have the others when they wake up from the nursery." It was a matter of principle among the guardians of the City that Utopian technology only be shared for peaceful purposes. Had the request had been for anything improper—weapons of war, perhaps, or enhanced means of interrogation for political prisoners—a man as angry as Friar Lorenz would not have failed to mention it. The friar accepted the flimsies with such obvious bad grace that Hanson added, "And Lorenz? Be sure to offer the man a cold drink, a hot meal, and a clean bed. It's a long ride from Portland; it's probably put him in a bad mood."

Caught by surprise, Friar Lorenz swallowed back a guffaw. "You're the boss."

"Please," Hanson said, turning away so the friar wouldn't see his face. "Never call me that."

~

So now here he was on the hillside, with a great big round harvest moon grinning down at him. The Wall surrounding what had formerly been called the City of God but was now merely the City still stood, but he could see three gaps in it from here, and there were many more, all guarded by brothers and sisters who had been trained to be the friendliest, most helpful people on earth—and to let no harmful technology past them on any account. The number of gaps would grow as the two orders of Guardians increased. Someday, the Wall would be gone entirely and cattle would browse beneath the City's flametrees.

Hanson took another swig from the jug—a long one—savoring the burning sensation of the alcohol as it flowed down his throat. Those two lovers that Becky had thrown up her hands in the air about, what should he recommend be done with them? If they were really and truly in love with each other, the answer would be simple: release them from their vows, give them enough money to make a new start in life (money was easy for Hanson to come by nowadays; of all the changes he had seen come to the world, this was the one he was least able to get used to), and encourage them to get married, make more brats, and be happy. But there seemed to be some doubt as to how they felt about each other. The Reverend Mother had written that she doubted they themselves knew. In which case, Hanson judged, forcing them into wedlock might well be the worst possible thing he could do to them.

It was a poser.

Sometime later, Hanson saw that there was somebody walking up the hill and realized that it was a woman. For a panicked instant, he thought it might be Becky, despite all her promises and assurances, come to see him in person, and half rose to his feet in alarm. Then she stumbled and recovered herself in way that told him that, no, this woman was never Becky but a stranger, and with mingled relief and apprehension, he settled back down onto the grass to await her arrival. It took a while, but at last she stood before him, looking nervous, as people who met Hanson for the first time tended to be. That was the disadvantage of being a legend; people reacted not to who you were but to who they imagined you to be.

The woman was young and lovely. There was a time when Hanson would have looked upon her with yearning. Now, however, what he felt was nostalgia. "Hello," she said. "Pardon me for interrupting you. They said not to. But my term of service here is over and I'm leaving in the morning, so . . ."

Hanson leaned over far to one side and patted the ground. "Have a seat."

The woman sat. "I hope you don't mind my clothing," she said, looking down at her loose, mannish trousers.

Hanson plucked at his robes. "Well, I never expected to find myself wearing a dress, neither. So I guess we're even, ai? What's your name?"

"Dr. Tyler. Mirriam. I'm from the South." She said this last almost defiantly, though the twin orders of Guardians had made it known that the citizens of all nations were welcome here. "Is there enough in that jug to share?"

"More'n enough, I reckon." Hanson passed it over.

Dr. Mirriam Tyler swiped her hand over the mouth, flipped the jug around so that it rested in the crook of her elbow, and took a swig. She gagged. "Oh, that is vile stuff!"

"If you don't want it . . ."

"I didn't say that." She took a second swig and, after a fit of coughing, handed it back. "Kind of grows on you."

"Ai." They sat in companionable silence for a while, neither willing to spoil the moment with words. When Hanson, who had been watching her closely out of the corner of his eye and every now and then taking another small sip of grain whiskey, judged that Dr. Tyler was stirring herself to speak at last, he said, "You're one of that group of scientists that's been studying the Cathedral, I s'pose."

"Scientists! Jumped-up mechanics is more like it. We ask questions, it answers us politely, we scratch our heads, we write it all down. Then we start over again. It's the scientific method, they tell me. Day after day after day, over and over, the exact same thing."

"I had a job like that once. Only 'stead of asking questions, I shoveled coal into a hole." Hanson leaned back on his arms, staring up at the cold, distant moon, more sensing than seeing Dr. Tyler looking at him quizzically as she tried to figure out if he were joking or not. He could have told her it was no joke but something dead serious. But if he started telling her his story now, it would be morning before he was half done with it. Meanwhile, he had some serious drinking to do. "You came here to ask me something, I s'pect."

"Oh! Yes. Yes, I did. I wanted to ask you . . ." Dr. Tyler was unaccountably flustered. Hanson wondered briefly if it was his renown or his office or something else. Then he realized that he didn't much care and downed another mouthful of alcohol. He'd been a legend back in the factory, too, in his youth, for how much work he could do; and that had been a much harder status to earn and a far more honest one. "You see, we're making such slow progress . . . and you only allow so many people in at a time . . . and there's so much to learn . . ." Her hesitant words suddenly coming together all in a rush, she said, "We don't take anything out but knowledge, which I'll grant you can be even more dangerous than Utopian technology, only it doesn't *have* to be, don't you see? We don't *have* to misuse knowledge, we can put it to good use. Oh, I'm making a mess of this! I had such good arguments lined up and now I can't think of a one."

"Just make your request," Hanson suggested gently. "Then I'll see what I can do."

"Let us bring more people in. Let us stay longer. Let us

actually learn from the City of God."

For a time Hanson was silent. Then he said, "I've got a problem of my own. Maybe you can help me with it." He noted the sharp, involuntary nod Dr. Tyler gave when he said that and for a second wondered if she were a fool. She was young, though, and sure of herself; in her world there were no problems without solutions, only those to which not enough thought had been applied. His world was exactly the opposite, and he wondered which of them was wrong. He hoped it was himself. "It's a tough one. The Reverend Mother Rebekah caught two young fools enthusiastically breaking their vows of celibacy. You understand what I'm saying, ai?" Dr. Tyler nodded. "Good. Now the situation can be handled one of two ways. If they're in love, they can be set free from their vows and given a little help finding a new place in life. But if they're not, well, they can be given the choice of leaving their orders or else staying but being made invisible to each other. We've got a device that will do that. We don't use it much, though.

"The problem is that the Reverend Mother doesn't know if they love each other. They don't know themselves. I for sure don't know. So how am I to choose the proper way of dealing with them, ai? You tell me that." By the time Hanson was done speaking, he could see that Dr. Tyler was quivering in her eagerness to share her answer with him. They were all so sure of themselves, these young people! Again, he wondered why he was in charge and not they. But that was a question to be pondered on another day. "Yes?"

"Let them decide for themselves!" Dr. Tyler said. "Explain to them about the treatment to make them invisible to each other. Then tell them that they'll have ten minutes of privacy in which to say goodbye. Put them in a room together and go away. Leave the back door unlocked. They'll find out if they love each other fast enough. Open the door when your ten minutes is up, and you'll know too."

Hanson laughed. "That a'n't half bad!" He thought about it and slapped his knee. "Not half bad at all! Let the young people sort it out for themselves. Maybe they'll make a hash of it, maybe not. Either way, it'll be their decision to make—not mine." He paused, made up his mind, and said, "So that's my answer to your question as well."

"How do you mean?"

"Nobody ever thought I could sit here forever, lording over who gets Utopian technology and who doesn't. *I* sure as hell didn't! But I figured if I could just slow down the way it oozed out, share it out equally, make sure that nobody got the upper hand over anybody else for long enough, there'd come a day when I wasn't needed anymore. Maybe that day's today."

All in a flash, Dr. Tyler was up on her feet, then down on her knees before Hanson. She seized his hands and would have kissed them if, embarrassed, he hadn't snatched them away from her. Reddening, he said, "You got your answer. Tell the boys below that from now on, as many scientists who want to come to the City, they can. So long as they don't take out anything more'n they can carry in their heads and notebooks. I'll write to Becky tomorrow, and if she agrees, as I s'pect she will, it'll be official."

The doctor, given more than she could possibly have expected, was grinning ecstatically, almost glowing with joy. So, before she could say anything more to embarrass him, Hanson said, "It's time for you to go now."

Dr. Tyler nodded wordlessly and turned away. Three steps down the hill, she spun about and said, "I want you to know how romantic it is, you and the Reverend Mother, working together but never meeting. Like Abelard and Heloise."

"I don't know who those are," Hanson said. Then, when Dr. Tyler had told him the entire story, "Well, I've grown as plump and harmless as a capon, so maybe that fits. Only, Becky was a'ways the smarter one of us two, so that don't. Also, she really a'n't Becky, you know. She does such of good job of being Becky that people forget that.

But I can't." He lurched to his feet. "But right now, Doctor, I'm going to shoo you away. I've got a lot of serious drinking to do. Plus, I've got to warn you that when I've poured enough alky into me, I start to singing, which by itself I reckon is a'right, my singing voice is good enough. But then I strip out of my robe and start to dance.

"And nobody wants to see an old fat man like me, dancing and singing naked in the moonlight."

Two Pilgrims on the Road to the City of God

Afterword by
Michael Swanwick

Long, long ago, when the world was young and dinosaurs still fell from the sky, I met Gardner Dozois. That was in 1974. I was long-haired, beardless, countercultural, and years away from publishing my first story. He was ex-army, bohemian, and the most celebrated writer known only to the cognoscenti in all of science fiction. I instantly became friends with his wife-to-be—after what she later and with characteristic wit called a "whirlwind seventeen-year courtship"—Susan Casper. Gardner was a little suspicious of me, afraid I would try to get him to read my undoubtedly terrible fiction.

There was little chance of *that* happening because, although I wrote persistently, madly, every day, I never managed to finish a story. I had no idea how to do that. But Susan and I palled around a lot, smoked dope, played pinball, argued the finer points of rock musicians, electronica, and Mummers clubs. On Thursday nights I hosted hearts games at my apartment on Twenty-Third

Street for a louche circle of acquaintances. Susan and I were both sharkish competitors, while Gardner and a young woman named Marianne Porter—remember that name—sat in the shadows talking.

Less than a year into our friendship, Susan entered the hospital for what she reassured everyone was "a silly little operation." The operation, of course, was neither silly nor little, and when she was wheeled off to the OR, she later said, she looked back at Gardner and saw from his face that he never expected to see her again. But shortly before, at one of the first science fiction conventions I ever attended, I had noted which people she talked to as friends and secretly got dozens of them to sign an outsized get-well card for her. So when, against all his fears, Susan emerged from surgery alive, Gardner decided that I was okay. Though he still worried I would inflict my admittedly terrible fiction upon him.

Back then, Gardner could be spotted from blocks away. He had long, straight blond hair that fell halfway down his back and a jaunty little beard and dressed in blue jeans, a black Stetson, and a black T-shirt with white block letters reading PROPHET OF DOOM. He and Susan were poor as church mice and had a child to provide for. Gardner's wonderful stories came slowly and with great effort and didn't bring in much money. So Susan held down a low-paying buzzkill of a job in Welfare while

Gardner supplemented their income by assembling anthologies and landing the occasional editorial gig. Once, his jeans split down the back, which was a major crisis because he didn't have a second pair or the cash on hand to buy one. He was a natural short fiction writer, but because novels paid better than short fiction, he made several abortive attempts at the form.

Among the projects begun and never finished was something called "the Digger Novel." Those in Gardner's literary cohort who had read that fragment spoke of it with awe. It began, they said, with a long, slow, mesmerizing description of a man shoveling coal into a hole, during which the reader got to see his life and soul destroyed—and then things got worse. It was, by repute, the best stick of prose Gardner had ever written. But he had snagged on a key plot point and the novel went unwritten, waiting for a burst of inspiration that, so far, had not come. Gardner was a private soul. I knew better than to ask if I could read it.

I also knew that I could never aspire to the first rank of Gardner's friends, people like Joe Haldeman and George R. R. Martin and Ed Bryant and George Alec Effinger and Jack Dann, writers who had begun their careers at roughly the same time, fought in the metaphoric trenches together, and written their best work hoping for each other's approval. This did not bother me. There are no chums like those of our youth. Also, they were like gods to me. Gardner was one of the pantheon of writers I revered and much older than me when we met. He had been published for years. He had the gravitas of age.

I was twenty-three years old and he was twenty-six.

Years passed. One day I was visiting Gardner and Susan in their tiny, cat-infested, three-rooms-and-a-bath apartment on Quince Street in Center City, Philadelphia. It was raining. Susan's son Christopher, who was angelically beautiful and engagingly mischievous, was running around underfoot. Susan had smoked the last of her Salem Light menthols and sent Gardner to the corner to buy another pack. (Sending each other on minor errands, like arguing frequently, was one way they expressed their love.) He shambled into the hallway, rooted around in the closet, and emerged with a raincoat and a cardboard box. Dumping the box in my lap, he said, "Here, Michael. This is the Digger Novel. You can read it while I'm out."

I was stunned. I had, without realizing it, passed some sort of threshold in our relationship and was now deemed worthy of the legendary text. I opened the box, lifted out the typescript, and began to read.

A few minutes later, Gardner came back with the cigarettes and returned the box to the closet. I forget how many pages I'd finished. Four, maybe, or five. It wasn't many.

More years passed.

They were punctuated periodically by visits from Jack Dann, who breezed down from Binghamton, New York, brimming with confidence and ambition. Jack was Gardner's closest and dearest friend back then and often came to Philadelphia to get his advice on whatever it was that Jack was then writing. Gardner or Susan would call me and we'd all go out to dinner together. Then we three writers (Susan later became a writer herself, and a good one, but at that time she looked upon us with tolerant amusement) would talk and argue and laugh deep into the night. Gardner and Jack would critique whatever I was working on, plan their own collaborations, plot the overthrow of all that was trite and boring about science fiction, and (inevitably) come up with a theme anthology to pitch to a New York publisher and then co-edit. Jack would give investment advice which neither Gardner nor I was in any position to benefit from. Ideas would fly from our brains like sparks, shooting up into a night sky more thronged with stars than anything ever painted by Van Gogh. We drank a lot of Gardner's cheap cream sherry.

After five years of dread that I'd impose my undeniably terrible fiction on him, curiosity got the better of Gardner and he asked to see something I'd written. That was the first, though far from the last, time I was invited to sit with Jack at Gardner's kitchen table. The two of them—who were, no exaggeration, the best story doctors in the business—took apart my manuscript and showed me how to turn it into a real story. And I got it! I really did. I reeled back to my apartment that evening at two A.M., up Spruce Street, past young men driving slowly by or sitting on stoops looking soulful or sauntering along the sidewalk, all checking one another out but not yet ready to commit, drunk on the realization that I was now an honest-to-goodness writer. Gardner and Jack had showed me how to do it. From that moment on, I knew that whatever I wrote would eventually be finished and that, while there might be rejections and even multiple rejections, it would all ultimately sell.

On another visit, we three started writing collaborative stories together. In the course of conversation, we'd toss out ideas, one would catch fire, and then, waving our arms excitedly and interrupting each other ("No, no, no, not the Big Bopper—*Buddy Holly*!"), we'd plot it out from start to finish, in a process much like the folktale about making stone soup. Add salt! Paprika! A wizard! Invisible cats! I would take detailed notes and, later, write the first draft and mail it to Jack, who would improve upon it and throw it to Gardner for the final polish. Tinker to Evers to Chance. We called ourselves the Fiction Factory. We wrote some wonderful stuff and sold it all, often to the slicks. One story sold to *Penthouse*. Another, which I had a very small part in writing and credit for which I turned down, appeared in *Playboy*. I learned a great deal on those nights. Including, yes, never to turn down credit in a story that will later sell to the best-paying fiction market in the country.

Years passed. They were filled with incident. For a while, I volunteered at the Wilma Project, sometime between its inception as a feminist theater collective and the massive success that Blanka and Jiri Zizka later made of it, during which I was one-half of the entire permanent staff—the one who put out the chairs and sold apples and hot cider at intermission. One sweltering Philadelphia summer, Gardner wrote his novel *Strangers* in crabbed longhand on yellow legal pads on an extremely short deadline—five weeks? nine?—sitting on a park bench in Washington Square in the shadow of Independence Hall. When I came to visit, Susan and I would pick him up at the park and go to dinner at the Midtown Diner, where we'd chat for an hour or two before releasing him into the darkness to stumble off, looking for a coffeehouse or unused set of steps where he could write. (David Hartwell, who had set the deadline, later told me there was no real need for it, but that he had doubted the book would be finished without the added pressure. I never shared that information with Gardner.) Philadelphia was a rougher place back then, with strip joints in the shadow of City Hall and streetwalkers in what is now the Gayborhood. Once, on South Street, Gardner saw a man stabbed to death with a fork. Another time, he was filmed crossing the street in front of the old Terminal Hotel for a shot in Brian De Palma's *Blow Out* that was later left on the cutting-room floor. Yet again, I saw a driver, for no discernible reason, swerve onto the sidewalk and attempt to run down Gardner and Susan.

Meanwhile, Marianne Porter and I had fallen in love. We were married in Tabernacle Church in West Philadelphia, whose congregation she belonged to and where I had the job of church secretary, with Gardner and Susan among those in attendance. My first two stories placed on the Nebula ballot, both in the novelette category. Back then, sagely, SFWA gave writers in that situation the option of withdrawing one story from the ballot. "You're not going to win," Gardner advised me, "so you might as well keep both on. It'll bring you more attention." Three years later, Marianne and I had a son, Sean. He and Gardner, who was always good with children, got along like a house afire. As an adult, Sean would work for a time as Gardner's office manager.

It was now the eighties. Gardner asked Jack and me to help him come up with a plot for the Digger Novel. He had brought Hanson all the way to the City of God and could go no further. He assumed that the people (there was never any doubt that they were people like any other, only obscenely wealthy) on the other side of the Wall were evil, aristocratic, and decadent. But Gardner, who knew so well what it was like to be a member of the underclass, had no idea what form that decadence would take.

Somewhere along the line, perhaps in preparation for this evening, perhaps earlier, I'd finally been allowed to read what had been written of the Digger Novel all the way through and was blown away by it. So I was thrilled at the possibility of being a footnote to literary history, the man who made its completion possible.

Jack and I spent the evening throwing out ideas by the handful, like so much spaghetti, hoping that something would stick to the wall. We came armed with multiple scenarios, each enthusiastically building upon the other's visions and spontaneously inventing new possibilities as the old ones were shot down. "Oh yeah!" Jack would say. "And then you could—" And I would gleefully add, "Absolutely! After which—" Gardner listened carefully to each idea, and then, like some great, shaggy beast, swung his head slowly from side to side. So we threw out more and more and more ideas. All to the same response.

It was clear that Gardner's subconscious, though it would not share this information with *him,* knew exactly what it wanted the story to be and none of our suggestions came anywhere near to hitting the mark. Back went the novel into the closet.

More years passed.

I came to accept that the Digger Novel would never be written.

With the unexpectedness of a lightning bolt (though later, in retrospect, it would seem inevitable) Gardner was named the new editor of *Isaac Asimov's Science Fiction Magazine*. The magazine's demands on his time were enormous. I stopped bringing my stories to him to critique. As did Jack. Gardner went on to become the most influential science fiction editor of his era, second in the common esteem only to John W. Campbell. During his nineteen-year tenure, he earned fifteen Hugo Awards for Best Editor. He also continued to edit *The Year's Best Science Fiction,* an enormous "bug crusher" (as Bruce Sterling characterized it) of a book whose compilation required that he read literally every SF story written each year. In part this was because he was convinced the *Asimov's* gig wouldn't last long. But also he wanted a good excuse to read every SF story written each year. The original publisher, Jim Frenkel, had to be talked out of publicizing it with the slogan, "We Have the Fattest Best of the Year—and the Fattest Editor Too!"

Gardner all but stopped writing.

But not quite. Above all else, Gardner valued being a writer. His two Nebula Awards for short fiction meant much more to him than the Hugos ever did. An editor could not channel the Promethean fire; he could only search for it in the slush pile and buy it when it appeared. Writers were the real thing. Somehow, though his stories would be rare as unicorns, they still appeared.

More years passed.

At the end of a visit to his new Society Hill apartment—a far cry from the Quince Street digs, with a fireplace and a Jacuzzi tub—Gardner saw me to the front stoop and then said, "Wait a second." He went inside and returned with a familiar cardboard box.

"I'm never going to write the Digger Novel," he said. "So you might as well take it and see if you can turn it into a novella."

I took the box from him. "I know exactly how to do this," I lied. "I'm not going to tell you now because I want it to be a surprise!" (Remember, I'd long ago given up on Gardner ever finishing it on his own.) I clutched the box to my chest and began to edge away, afraid that Gardner would come to his senses and snatch it back.

"It's clear to me this isn't going anywhere," he said unhappily. "So you might as well make something of it."

I was down to the sidewalk. "Wait until you see what I have in mind! You'll love it!"

Gardner wasn't listening. In his heart of hearts, he was mourning the necessity to hand over the child of his imagination to me. "But I'll tell you what," he said. "Make the conclusion open-ended. Just in case we decide to make a novel of it."

"You must be reading my mind!" I chirped.

Miraculously, in that instant, even as I was saying those words, the solution entered my mind: Hanson would enter the City of God and find it abandoned. The people are gone, following the consequences of their decadence into unknown realms. But their toys remain.

And those toys are dangerous.

I made the City as menacing and hallucinatory as I could. Gardner and I swapped the manuscript back and forth, improving it with every pass, and when the story was done to both our satisfactions, he made the polish draft. Because Gardner was a master stylist, he always did the final draft on all the collaborations, whether with me or with others. We all agreed he was the best.

After a great deal of to-and-froing, we agreed to name the story "The City of God." It appeared in *Omni Online,* edited by Ellen Datlow, and, months later, in *Asimov's Science Fiction.* (Gardner recused himself and Sheila Williams made the decision to buy it.) We couldn't have been happier with how it had turned out.

Still. Gardner had put the idea of a novel into our

heads. We often talked over the possibility of writing two more novellas, "The City of Angels" and "The City of Man," which could be combined with the first, continuing Hanson's saga. Each novella would be published independently and then we would merge all three into one continuous narrative and sell it as a novel. It was a solid plan. But we kept putting it off.

Years passed.

Both Gardner and I had things to do. Pressing matters of magazines to put out and anthologies to compile and stories and novels and essays to write. Gardner and Susan got married and bought a house. Their son, Christopher, and his wife, Nicole, had two children, Tyler and Isabella, whom the newly minted grandparents loved without reservation. A taxi accident put Gardner in the hospital, and since neither the cab company nor his insurance wanted to pay for it, he had to deal with lawyers for what seemed forever and was literally years. Some time after that, Susan's health, never good to begin with, took a severe turn for the worse. She was in and out of physical rehab for years.

Because Susan could no longer handle the stairs, they rented out their house and moved into an apartment. Gardner sold his enormous collection of books, about which Pulitzer Prize-winning critic Michael Dirda once exclaimed, "These are the most delightfully *read* books

I've ever seen!", to a fan. His papers went to the University of California, Riverside, and Gardner threw in several of the uglier of his many Hugos as a lagniappe. When he was moving from the one location to the other, somebody asked what he wanted done with a box of the remaining Hugos. "You want one? Take it!" he said. "Take as many as you like."

He meant it.

Through all of this, Gardner and I continued, off and on, to talk about the City of God Novel (its name changed with the first novella) and where it might go. "It's hard to talk about a novel that hasn't been written yet, that may never be," Gardner said when we were in the early stages of working out the final plot. "But I dimly see Hanson as ultimately being left with some sort of gatekeeper or overseer responsibility for the rest of humanity that he didn't really want and didn't really think he was doing a good job at." Then he came to what, to him, was the heart of the novel: "The only thing that keeps him from becoming as corrupt as everybody else is the knowledge of how bad it looks from the lower depths when you allow yourself to be transformed into a boss, and sort of a determination not to have that happen to him." It was important to Gardner that Hanson remain, now and forever, a blue-collar guy, a worker, a decent man of simple tastes who had no desire whatsoever to make others suffer.

Gardner made a start on "The City of Angels," chronicling Hanson's imprisonment. I thought it was brilliant and extended the plot, returning Hanson to the City of God. Susan Casper's health, meanwhile, worsened precipitously. Marianne and I visited her at their apartment one day, bringing with us Samuel Delany, who was an old friend and whose visit cheered her enormously. Chip (as Delany is known to his friends) took a picture of the three of us that was to be her last. That night, in her sleep, she passed peacefully away. Gardner kept the box with her ashes on the windowsill of their apartment. "It's silly," he said, "because I know that she's not there or anywhere else and can't hear me, but sometimes I'll still talk to her as if she were."

He said that at the Pen and Pencil, America's oldest journalists' club, on Latimer Street, where he was a member. The widowed women among our cronies told Gardner how he was going to feel now and in the future and he listened to them with attentive respect, prepping himself for life alone. His old friend Pat Cadigan flew in from London to do her bit to comfort him. Her original intent had been to visit Susan, but mortality descended before the flight could be arranged. I'll carry with me forever the memory of Pat and Gardner sitting on his couch together, holding hands and smiling through their sadness, saying nothing because there was nothing that needed to be said.

It was in the lead-up to this difficult time, while Susan was still alive, that Gardner and I finally got serious about the City of God Novel, talked out the plot, and started working steadily on the second novella.

There is a sentimental notion, among many of Gardner's friends, that without Susan he had lost the will to live. This makes Marianne mad enough to spit. He had not. Our son, Sean, who was working for him at the time, reported that Gardner was constantly busy assembling anthologies, coaxing new stories out of writers, and, of course, actively at work on the novel he and I had intended for decades. He had plans for the future and things he wanted to do. He had begun and abandoned a sequel to *Strangers*, and I am convinced that, given time, he could have been coaxed into finishing it. Alas, he was not given time.

He died with "The City of Angels" halfway finished.

Gardner had gone into Pennsylvania Hospital with congestive heart failure and was expected to make a complete recovery. But a hospital is a very dangerous place to be. Five times they delayed his release. Then he caught an opportunistic systemic infection. Christopher had retired from the army with the rank of major, and he and Nicole had moved nearby so they could look after his parents. Now he emailed me to say that if I wanted to see Gardner, I should do it quickly because he wasn't expected to last the weekend. Marianne and I rushed to his bedside. His large, strangely inert body was unconscious, pallid, still. The next day we came to visit again and found his family gathered there. Gardner's sister, Gail, told me that he had always been her protector. Christopher said that the decision had been made to take Gardner's body off life support. They were waiting for one last relative to arrive before letting him pass away.

Much as we loved him, Marianne and I knew that his last moments belonged to his family, and not to us. So although Christopher invited us to stay, we did not. Marianne bent down and kissed Gardner's forehead. I placed my hand over his and, too quietly for anybody else to hear, said, "Goodbye, old friend." Then I turned away, with that same hand clutched over my eyes to hide the tears that I could not manage to stanch. Tears identical to those that are running down my face even now, as I write these words.

I drove us home. Sometime not long after, Gardner left the planet.

~

In the wake of Gardner's death, I knew that the third novella, "The City of Man," would never be written. I could do a reasonable imitation of his rich, wonderful style, but without his input, his passion, his inspiration, the novella would just be . . . mine. I had no desire to see all that we'd put into the text diminished like that.

Nevertheless, I wanted the world to experience the ending that Gardner had planned and obsessed over for decades. I wanted everyone to know that the man who had a reputation as a very gloomy writer indeed had come up with a happy—no! joyous!—ending. And I wanted to give him one last novel.

So I took the half-written "City of Angels," dropped the title and much of the intended plot, and moved it in a direction that would bring it to Gardner's intended conclusion. When it was finished, I appended it to "The City of God," and then broke the combined text into chapters, so that it would read continuously as one story, the novel it was always meant to be, instead of appearing as two novellas. Finally, I went over the whole thing, giving it the final polish draft Gardner would have and striving to make it sound as much like him as possible. In this, I think I succeeded. But that's a judgment for the reader to make, not me.

Lee Harris at Tor.com liked the novel and bought it. He did, however, gently observe that "The City of God," while a fine title for a novella, was perhaps not the right one for the book. It took several weeks of agony and bafflement—this is normal for book titles, by the way; they can be the most difficult part of writing—to come up with something that worked. Never had I missed Gardner more. It would have been great fun to brainstorm the title with him, throwing out possibilities and hooting scornfully at the lamer attempts. But at last, in a dream, I saw the words "City Under the Stars" on the front page of the typescript, and they felt right to me.

This is not the novel that Gardner and I started to write a quarter century ago, much less the one he set out to create more than twenty years before *that*. But I am proud of it. Also, I know that Gardner would be tickled to have one last novel on his bibliography. Let this stand as a memorial to him.

Gardner Dozois was the kindest man I ever met. He was also one of the most modest. Many a time I wished he were less so. "Nobody wants to meet an old fat man!" he would say when Marianne and I nagged him into attending some social event where, of course, he was the belle of the ball and charmed the pants off of everybody. In his last years, whenever anyone talked about his legacy, he would scoff, "I'll be forgotten five minutes after I'm dead. Nobody is going to give a damn about an old fat man!"

In this, he was wrong. Gardner left behind many, many friends, and they all took his passing hard. I, for one, miss him terribly.

So would you, if you had met him.

About the Authors

MICHAEL SWANWICK published his first story in 1980, making him one of a generation of new writers that included Pat Cadigan, William Gibson, Connie Willis, and Kim Stanley Robinson. In the third of a century since, he has been honored with the Nebula, Theodore Sturgeon, and World Fantasy Awards and received a Hugo Award for fiction in an unprecedented five out of six years. He also has the pleasant distinction of having *lost* more major awards than any other science fiction writer.

Roughly one hundred fifty stories have appeared in *Amazing, Analog, Asimov's, Clarkesworld, High Times, New Dimensions, Eclipse, Fantasy & Science Fiction, Interzone, The Infinite Matrix, Omni, Penthouse, Postscripts, Realms of Fantasy, Tor.com, Triquarterly, Universe,* and elsewhere. Many have been reprinted in Best of the Year anthologies, and translated into Japanese, Croatian, Dutch, Finnish, German, Italian, Portuguese, Russian, Spanish, Swedish, Chinese, Czech, and French. Several hundred works of flash fiction have been published as well.

A prolific writer of nonfiction, Swanwick has published book-length studies of Hope Mirrlees and James Branch Cabell as well as a book-length interview with Gardner Dozois. He has taught at Clarion, Clarion West, and Clarion South. He was guest of honor at MidAmeriCon II, the 2016 World Science Fiction Convention.

Swanwick is the author of ten novels, including *In the Drift* (an Ace Special), *Vacuum Flowers, Stations of the Tide, The Iron Dragon's Daughter, Jack Faust, Bones of the Earth, The Dragons of Babel, Dancing with Bears,* and *Chasing the Phoenix.* His short fiction has been collected in *Gravity's Angels, A Geography of Imaginary Lands, Moon Dogs, Tales of Old Earth, Cigar Box Faust and Other Miniatures, The Dog Said Bow Wow, The Best of Michael Swanwick,* and *Not So Much, Said the Cat.* His most recent novel, *The Iron Dragon's Mother,* completes a fantasy trilogy begun almost twenty-five years ago.

He lives in Philadelphia with his wife, Marianne Porter.

~

GARDNER DOZOIS is widely regarded as one of the most important editors in the history of science fiction. His editorial work earned more than forty Hugo Awards, forty Nebula Awards, and thirty Locus Awards, and he was awarded the Hugo for Best Professional Editor fifteen times between 1988 and his retirement from *Asimov's* in 2004, having edited the magazine for almost twenty years! He also served as the editor of *The Year's Best Science Fiction* anthologies and coeditor of the *Warrior* anthologies, *Songs of the Dying Earth,* and many others. As a writer, Dozois twice won the Nebula Award for best short story. He was inducted into the Science Fiction Hall of Fame in 2011 and received the Skylark Award for Lifetime Achievement. Gardner was actively writing and editing when he died in the spring of 2018. Recent publications include two nonfiction collections, *Sense of Wonder* and *On the Road with Gardner Dozois* (with an introduction by Michael Swanwick), three anthologies, *The Year's Best Science Fiction: 35th Annual Collection, The Book of Magic,* and *The Very Best of the Best: 35 Years of The Year's Best Science Fiction,* several short stories in *Asimov's* and *F&SF,* and a podcast of "A Special Kind of Morning" on *LeVar Burton Reads.*

Lightning Source UK Ltd.
Milton Keynes UK
UKHW010630230123
415808UK00006B/1174